HOMOLAND

HOMOLAND

A Novella By
SAM JENKS

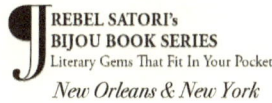

REBEL SATORI's
BIJOU BOOK SERIES
Literary Gems That Fit In Your Pocket
New Orleans & New York

Published in the United States of America by
Rebel Satori Press
www.rebelsatoripress.com

Paperback ISBN: 978-1-60864-397-4

Cover Design: Daniel Sheen
Author Photo: Misk Ridd

Acknowledgements:
Steve Benson for his part in our collaborative nonfiction outline 'Homolands' developed in 2023 as part of the Queerscapes Project, which inspired not just the title but was an early exploration for me of many of the themes in this work.

James Leahy, John Lugo Trebble and Steven Benson for reading early drafts and gifting me their insights.

Hey honey skin.
I'm here now.
I've traded in my roof and my regular tricks
To do with you what Robinson didn't dare.
You with your troubled beauty
I'm gonna bring you to your knees,
Rip out that heart of amber.

Chapter 1

I flip up the collar of my shirt so that it cups my pale babyface – my twenty-four passes as seventeen. I smooth my cream cords across the contours of my crotch and stride toward the front door.

At the door, I run a comb through my hair, still bouffant from my last project. The glow of my shirt reflects in the door's frosted glass panel. I ring the doorbell - the standard soft chime. After a few seconds, my reflection darkens as a silhouette from the other side approaches.

I take a deep breath, the door opens.

There he is. Taller, wirier than me. Mismatched denim shirt and jeans. Short wavy hair, stubbly chin.

'Hello?' His tone is neutral.

'Ben? It's Manfried, from Naked City; we met online.'

His eyes seem to reach out for more.

'Flaneurs International.' I add.

There's a bolt of recognition in those soft brown eyes - his hand slides down the edge of the doorframe and catches on the latch, 'Fuck!' he exclaims, and in one reflex presses his thumb onto the cut finger. Already a drop of blood.

His face is pained, 'Hi, Manfried, but?'

I'm on edge too, the moment has power. I study his face, frozen, scared even. Definitely less confident than when we chatted online. Don't freak him out now, there's no Plan B.

I slide my hands into the deep pockets of my elephant cords and open out my shoulders in submission, 'Call me Manny.'

'Manny, but, but you're here?'

'You said you were pretty much available anytime.'

A panic darts across his eyes like a meteor burning across the night.

'I know we chatted a lot online, Manfried, err Manny, but to turn up on my doorstep?'

'You sounded pretty desperate, Ben.'

'How did you find me?'

'You told me where you were, more or less.'

Ben puffs air out through his lips, glances over his shoulder back into the house.

I look up at Ben through a strand of hair that has dropped across my eyes, and in my softest voice, 'Have I done something wrong here?'

Ben looks down at me and I capture his brown eyes in that vital moment.

He steps back, points to the front room, 'Look, you better come in a minute.'

He glances at my trainers.

I give him my best apologetic face, 'I better take these off. I had to do the last bit cross-country.'

Ben takes my small backpack as I remove my red trainers which are flecked with dry mud, and, on

2

further calculation, my socks. He points to a rug near the door with other shoes on it. Some look like the unexpected old woman's, who I saw in the garden when I was watching the house just before.

The front room is neat and tidy. I take the beige sofa in front of the window, the sun floods through the flowering pink magnolia in the front garden, projecting a soft undulating negative onto the white walls.

Ben takes the wine red sofa opposite me, a low coffee table divides us. Ben gives me an almost stern look,

'Look, I think there's maybe been a misunderstanding.'

'Seems like it.'

I hear voices coming from a radio at the back of the house and I shift my eyes in that direction.

Ben reads me, 'Oh it's Mum. She'll be in the conservatory listening to The Archers. She always does that after lunch before dropping off.'

'You said you lived alone.'

He squirms, but as he's about to open his mouth I raise my hand, 'It doesn't matter, really.'

I relax into the sofa, tired from my journey, gradually sliding downwards, my legs splaying, allowing myself a moment of self enjoyment as I watch myself flex my toes.

Ben glances towards the kitchen, 'Would you like a drink of something?'

I decide it's best to keep him here in this room.

I point to the bottles on a retro sideboard, 'You say Whyte and Mackay is your favourite, yes?'

Ben initially pushes both his hands under his thighs but good manners gets him on his feet.

As Ben fixes the drinks; I size him up, boy next door type, maybe more than meets the eye. Sadly, his battered white crocs leave too much to the imagination, the shape of his feet obliterated like censored cock on some Japanese pornsites.

He passes me a tumbler containing a good slug of whisky.

He's on edge, I can tell, it gives me a thrilling tingle in the back of my neck, like I shouldn't be here, and that he's already an accomplice.

He raises his glass, 'Cheers.'

'Cheers.' I take a sip, feel the heat first on my lips, then I let it roll in my mouth, the smooth tones power through like a flooded stream about to burst its banks, 'Good stuff.'

Ben takes a breath, 'Sorry, you turning up like this, it's caught me by surprise.'

'When we chatted online – you made a deep impression – your problem with the city.'

Ben looks away for a second. 'Did I come across that strong?'

'It's how I read it - we chatted for hours about a joint project to get to the heart of it.'

'I suppose we did.'

'So that's why I'm here.' I say, taking another sip.

'But, that's online talk.'

4

'I don't have a separate online persona.' I snap.

Ben's shoulders slump, he's so fragile, 'It's all true, what I said. I'm not some psycho-stalker freak. You saw my website, landscapes, bits of art, a new psychogeography, though I'm gonna ditch that term – but it's what I do. I was always coming this way, this city interests me, you interest me.'

He looks undecided so I do it for him.

'It won't cost you anything, except your time of course, if you have any to spare.' I add, knowing full well he does.

His chest looks tense, his breathing shallow, constricted by that cheap denim shirt. Slow down, let him catch up.

'Where did you come from, today I mean?' Ben asks.

I run my fingers carefully through my hair. 'London – I've not long finished a short project around Piccadilly and Soho, working with an artist. I've just uploaded it all onto my website if you want to have a look sometime.'

'Err, OK, sure.'

'It was a bit of a different project to ours, those methods won't work here. We'll have to come up with something different to get to the bottom of this place.'

'How did you get over here?'

'Hitched, got dropped off in some hamlet a few miles away, then took the old paths. I'm here now.' I recline a touch more, stretch my legs out and watch my toes as they uncurl in the afternoon sun; and at last

I think he's really noticing me.

I look down into my drink but I can still see Ben looking at me over the rim of his glass - I feel the heat of his gaze sliding up my thighs. I gift him more time to savour me.

Ben breaks the silence, 'So Manny is short for Manfried. It's an interesting name,'

'I suppose. It was given me by the woman who had me or someone else around at the time, nobody is quite sure.' I enjoy watching those words cut into his facial expression.

He weighs this up and decides to probe, 'Where're you from originally?'

I yawn at the triviality, 'Not from around here, you neither, I don't think. It's a good start that, us both being outsiders.'

Ben changes tack. 'Are you really a student of Robinson, I thought he was just an imaginary character in Patrick Keiller films?'

So his brain has clicked into gear – well I'm prepared.

'You'll need to talk to Keiller about that. The Robinson I know is for real.'

I empty my glass and casually look at the bottle on the coffee table. Ben picks up on it and pours me another shot.

I've seen enough of Ben to know what he needs. I imagine my fingers twisting his hair, I feel my cock thickening.

I take another sip, lean back and close my eyes.

I visualise Ben staring at my crotch with his starved eyes right now. I listen to the silence in the room, I'm sure Ben is holding his breath. I rub my thumb on my glass slowly. I hear him swallow. I caress my crotch with the base of the tumbler before moving the tumbler to one side. I count to five in my head then snap open my green blue eyes. He's a mouse caught in a cat's claws. Ben pales and becomes still. Playing dead won't help him now. I tune our breathing – as my chest rises, his follows. Our heartbeats aligned. A bead of sweat emerges like precum onto his temple – he's mine.

'So you're free for the next few days?'

'Possibly, yeah. I'm not working at the moment, but, yeah, probably.'

I part my lips slightly, 'Yes, or?'

'Yes.'

I place my drink on the table, 'Let me get this right about you and this place. You feel like an outsider?' That last word always turns me on.

Ben nods.

'Impotent; like in a power way?' I ask.

He replies with a more hesitant nod.

My cock is hard for his benefit not my pleasure, there's no wetness there. A part of me wants to run my hands across him right now to get to know that part of his subconscious that even he doesn't know. I have a theory that the subconscious moves around the body, hiding.

When I bodyscanned that guy in the art cube in

Piccadilly, it had been different from the other times. It's as if I'd clicked how to do it properly and since then I've been desperate to do it again.

Ben looks towards the back of the house, as if he's worried about 'Mum' appearing at the door. It doesn't concern me, if anything it adds to the thrill.

I look at his crotch - he's hard. I let my look linger.

Ben gulps.

Calculations complete, no need to fish for kinks yet. I drop his eyes and get to my feet, straightening out my cords, my hardness already receding, 'OK. I think this project is underway.'

'What do you mean?' asks Ben, stumbling over his own words.

'I need to go and check-in at my accommodation. I'll message you tomorrow – you can take me for a walk around the city.'

When he opens the front door, I move close enough to feel the heat of his breath.

'Don't worry, Ben, this project is going to be fun.'

I step through the door and head for the Art School. Time to do my research.

Chapter 2

I slide on the white cotton gloves - it feels like I'm participating in someone else's kink. The book rests unopened on the reading-stand in front of me. I go with the urge to run my fingertip down the vertically arranged title, silver inlaid into the rippled blue cover - pressing down to feel the hard smooth letters.

Here at the Art School, the librarian had hesitated to retrieve 'Chronostasis' from the Artbook Collection – I didn't have a library card – but the fact that I knew of the book's existence swayed her. When she placed it on the bookstand she commented on the beautifully crafted traditional Japanese book binding, the handmade paper. As she passed me the protective gloves she said that only a few copies had been made and they wanted this single copy to have a long life in their collection. I bowed my head respectfully and satisfied with my deference she left me to it.

I carefully open the book, it is laid out with a monochrome photo on the left hand pages – each complemented by a few lines of Ben's writing on the facing pages. The art photographer is someone called Riku. I pause at Riku's very staged self portrait – a young guy in dark denim, wearing a bowler hat, sits next to a desk dominated by a portable typewriter but also strewn with books and papers. Behind the desk, a case displaying books, postcards and two vintage cameras. Behind him, a dark jacket and a single white shirt hang in an open-sided wardrobe.

I wonder how this collaboration came about. Was desire, infatuation or sex part of the equation? Where is this guy now? I don't want to be competing.

I look closely at Riku's image. His face has a fine, delicate outline. Curtain hair hides half of each eye, the film's exposure has virtually bleached out his nose and mouth, though two dark pupils remain. He looks like some sort of woodland pixie – from another time – a lost look in his eyes. As I work my way through the book it's as if this Riku is trying to capture a past sense of British culture, but he's somehow got trapped there.

But I'm here to understand Ben – through his words – and I read them slowly. Page after page, I'm left with the sense that like the photographs, Ben's writing is dreamy, unanchored. I'm drawn to that lostness and I'm convinced now that if these words in any way reflect the writer, then Ben is the ideal accomplice for my project.

I finish the book and get ready to leave – I put in my ear buds and select one of my playlists – I'm about to take off the gloves, but something is niggling at me. Riku. I find him hot and I don't like that. What effect is he still having on Ben?

I reopen Chronostasis and return to his self-portrait. Bubblegum pop bursts into my ears 'Sugar

Baby love…'

I imagine Ben and this bitch talking about Barthes' Camera Lucida, flirtatiously debating the emotional effects of photography on the spectator. I remember the singer in my ears, his clockwork orange smile, his blond hair flowing out from underneath an oversized white cloth cap. I imagine Ben and Riku editing each other's work, leaning over each other's shoulders, brushing each other's ears with caffeinated breath. Later, they're in a pub, sharing a joke, Riku's face reddened from trying the local scrumpy that Ben recommended, relaxing, opening up.

'Oh oh oh.' croons the backing band.

I scan the room, there's no one around.

I gob onto Riku's face.

I watch as my saliva soaks into Riku's smooth skin.

I sing along quietly, 'I never meant to hurt you oh oh oh.'

Curse completed, I close the book and head back to my hostel.

Chapter 3

I wake to a close-up view of a dusty green curtain. The youth hostel dorm is an overheated room with 8 beds, all empty except for mine, lingering the musk of the bodies that are now up and out.

I hadn't been able to sleep at first – so I fed my dopamine craving by scrolling dog videos on insta but I'd forgotten to turn off Grindr – that led to a bathroom at the back of the building – that led to a cute guy in his forties and £60. And the workout helped me get my zeds after.

I crack open the curtain and peer through the sash window – sloping parkland. My eye catches on a glint of light from a mirrored cube the size of a tea chest, sitting under a broad tree. Art. It starts me thinking about the project with Roy, which is where this all started.

Last Autumn, in an attempt to feed an urge to hang out more with people of my own age, and maybe make friends with people with serious money, I found a bar popular with art students from Central St Martins.

I kept going back, fascinated by the bohemian masks the students were shaping for themselves. With a whisky in hand, I would smile and edge my way into one of these arty groups but they soon discovered

I had nothing to talk about, and barring the occasional shag, I knew I was being kept at a distance, an outsider.

However, one night, I pulled a lecturer, Department of Sculpture. In bed the next morning we'd watched a film on his BFI Player, 'London', about an unseen and enigmatic psychogeographer called Robinson, who through his endless walks, maps the city in his own way. I felt an instant connection with this Robinson who, like me, existed on the fringes. I lapped up the accompanying bedroom seminar and soon, after looking deeper into the whole thing, began making a new mask for myself metaphorically made from pages of the Robinson myth and fused with the lecturer's cum. I had invented a story to tell, one that would have me accepted.

After a hollow Christmas where trading on mens' fantasies of Factory Apprentice had reached a new level of boredom; opportunity appeared online on a Royal College of Art student bulletin board.

'Artists Wanted: Make the switch between an experience of normal life and art.' – I was hooked – 'Use Space 03 as a base to explore the area, collect materials, find connections, carry out your art practice whilst fulfilling your basic human needs. Engage, interact, participate, co-author.'

And money was involved.

Ripping off Debord, I set up my artist website, 'Naked City', falsely claiming a collaboration with an indie artists collective in Manchester.

It got me through the door. Roy was a calm,

friendly PhD student with a round face and a mass of jet black hair dyed copper. At night, under street lighting, he looked like his head was on fire. He insisted on being called Roy though his website had his first name as Yihang. We got on. I could make him laugh, but he also listened to what I had to say and he said he believed in me.

Within weeks I found myself transported to Space 03, a 3mx3mx3m white cube, temporarily sited next to Eros in Piccadilly Circus, my studio and home for a week.

From the get go, I would set off on meandering walks, reacquainting myself with the district. The more I walked the more I seemed to sink into the landscape, centimetre by centimetre, strata by strata. It didn't take too long to reach the late 1950s. No need for carbon 14 dating – I'd ghosted into something between a 'Dilly rent boy and a young Cliff Richard.

I scoured the nearby boutiques and bought the look with my art 'fund' – the drainpipe suit, the bouffant hair, the Lucky Strike cigarettes. And one evening, loitering outside the cube, I'd met this guy dressed up like James Dean and that's when it had all gotten weird.

I'd been attracted by his scrutinising eyes and the perfection of his outfit – the jeans, white t-shirt and red baseball blouson all perfectly set off by the pompadour hair – 1950s America through and through. It turned out he was a Tokyo company man on holiday. I'd invited him into the cube, sex was the only thing on the agenda, sex as art in this case. I kinda wish I hadn't.

He got off on being restrained in his Americana, jeans around his ankles, t-shirt pulled over his head. I was getting off on the fact that Roy would be able to watch the action back on the Space 03 CCTV footage, maybe even live for all I knew. And, just like with anyone that intrigues me and we've got intimate, my hands took over and I scan-tripped him.

I'd discovered scan-tripping, as I called it, at thirteen, when I once dreamily explored my own body, unearthing a vision of being a lost and hungry toddler on a deserted building site.

A few years later, when I started sex working, I played with my new found skill and refined it. Now I just see it as part of my personality - like being kind or caring.

But that evening with Jimmy Dean, it felt too powerful. My head had seared with the black and white image of an East-Asian looking man dressed in an immaculate tuxedo suit, he had a frail Fred Astaire look, hands clasped together. He stood next to a much taller white military guy in khaki, hands on his hips. My hands had recoiled and I'd blinked hard in an effort to focus on something else. This trip had scared me, darker than anything else I'd experienced, as if I had gone through him, beyond him somehow.

Swept along with the flow of our sex, I complied with his plea to stub out my cigarette on his chest. As we sipped Suntory whisky after, he told me cigarette

15

kink had been a James Dean thing. All I saw was a red sun. I sit up and shake my head in an effort to discard the image and drag myself back into now.

Focus on the day ahead. Everything has got to be tight, there can't be any gaps in my story.

Chapter 4

I'm on the canal path towards Ben's. I see his house, halfway up the hill on the other side of the river. I think about our conversations since we met online. My story holds so far, but I need to find out what he's reading - I need to stay ahead.

I take a path which drops down from the towpath and through a short tunnel under the railway. I think about Ben's skepticism about Robinson, he's going to ask more questions for sure and I'm not sure how to play it.

Robinson picked me up in Soho towards the end of my time in the Cube. His financial situation, reflected in a low paid job in further education meant he could only afford to bring me back and pay for my escort services the once.

When I told him about how I'd used Space 03, he'd connected my channelling the area to his ideas on psychogeography. I was interested in his book collection. We came to an arrangement and I ended up staying a few weeks. I'd let him shape the sex he wanted - and unusually for me, I also let him play at moulding me to what he wanted.

I stop on a footbridge crossing the river and look down into the slowly moving murky water.

Robinson poured key writers into me, Benjamin, Blake, and Rimbaud, Breton, Debord, Defoe, Edgar Allen Poe. Whilst on long walks, he geolocated them in London for me. I got to see the city as he saw it.

I read what I could even though I'm not bright that way and I'm sure it's all jumbled up. But one thing became clear, Robinson was an observer, his analysis of the city through these writers was impressive, but he didn't seem to want to do anything about it. The more I pushed him on this the more defensive he got. I wanted to know why psychogeographers couldn't use this knowledge to change things for the better, take on power, undermine it.

Now back in honeyed stone suburbia, I push on up the hill towards Ben's.

I remember that day when Robinson and I were out walking, crisscrossing London between places Rimbaud had been known to live. I started on again about taking action and he snapped back, 'Why don't you set up another of your rent-boy standard scams to prove your point?' That was some shade, but from that day on, I was on it.

Robinson was intrigued that I'd chosen this particular little city. Sure, the positives were that it was overwhelmingly white, middle-class, mono-cultural and not too big, he said. But on the other hand he'd wondered if anything had ever happened there since the Georgian period. All in all though, he knew I was going to do it.

When it came to it, when I was building up the

courage to say I was ending our arrangement, he went into his cluttered wardrobe, dragged out an old shoebox and passed it to me.

'Your trainers have had it, will you wear these?' The red Adidas Gazelles.

My eyes lit up. I remember sitting on his bed and him on his knees in front of me.

'I wore them years ago, first edition I think, they'll last forever. Go on, try them on.'

I couldn't be sure if he had worked me out – because I'd kept that kink hidden from him but he hit bullseye with this gift.

Chapter 5

Ben answers the door in crumpled jogging bottoms and a University of California sweatshirt - his sleepy biscuit odour reaches me and makes me want to get closer.

'Hi Manny. You said you'd text,' his voice is dry and groggy.

I take out my mobile, 'I did, look.'

Ben shakes his head in defeat, 'One minute ago?'

Her voice booms out from the back of the house, 'Who's that?'

Ben looks back over his shoulder, his hulk of a Mum, draped in an oriental silk dressing gown, fills the doorway at the other end of the corridor. Her mass of permed grey-blond hair almost touches the top of the doorframe.

'This is Manny I was telling you about.' says Ben.

'Hello, I'm June, have you got time for a cuppa?'

Ben rolls his eyes, 'I'm not ready yet anyway.'

I call back to her, 'Yes please, we've got time.'

The kitchen opens out into a conservatory, Ben's Mum points me towards a white plastic table whilst she makes a pot of tea. Ben helps her. I look around – a few scraggly potted geraniums on the windowsills. A bird of paradise, orange flowers dying, stands on the floor near a french door, in an ornate and cobwebbed ceramic pot.

When we're all seated, I see her dressing gown is a print of cherry blossomed branches with small songbirds perched here and there.

She puffs out her chest, 'As I was just telling him, I had a dream last night that there was a stranger in the house.'

'And here I am.' I say.

'But you were here yesterday weren't you, as well?' she probes.

My chest tenses slightly and I look across at Ben thinking, jeez, what do we have here?

'I could smell the mud.' she says.

'OK, Mum.' Ben's trying to calm her.

'You're like the Japanese boy.' says Mum.

No I'm not, I think to myself.

'Mum, his name is Riku, as you well know.'

She ploughs on. 'But he never showed his face here. 'Manny.' she muses, 'Is that after Byron's Manfried, Defoe's Man Friday or is it just an implication, you know boy-man or mannish girl?

'Mummm!' Ben looks at me apologetically.

'And your name?' I ask.

She looks taken aback but she answers anyway, 'June.'

I'm not sure we're going to get on. She's not important anyway, Ben's the one I need. I idly look out into the garden. A geriatric tree dominates a small patch of stressed lawn, surrounded by overgrown borders tinged in blue.

'Is that King Apple, from Chronostasis?' I ask, then watch the colour drain out of Ben's face.

Ben gasps, 'Yes, yes it is. But?'

'I read it yesterday. I remember you telling me that the art school had a copy. How does it go – 'I often daydreamed that he might hold within his rings a record of the longings of those that gazed into his branches.' – I like that thought.'

June hums.

'Thank you. Though it's not typical of my writing. Riku, the artist, photographer, he'd become obsessed with late Victorian romanticism.' Ben blusters.

I'm feeling vindictive. 'Yeah it works as a romantic piece.'

June slurps her tea then chuckles, 'He's long gone, back to Japan.'

Ben holds onto his mug with both hands. Was he regretting missed moments with Riku, or had he just creeped the poor guy out? I went with my instincts. 'I noticed he had a copy of Breton's Nadja in one photo, a bit of a stalker classic of surreal, flaneur fiction.'

Ben looks down at the floor, embarrassed. He's no need to be, I'm a bit of a fan of stalking – I like the sexual undertow – that's partly what's brought me here.

'Yes, I didn't notice that book featured until recently.' Ben admits.

'Anyway', June asks, 'what's your project about, here?'

I roll out the official version, 'Ben and I are

members of an online group, Flaneurs International, about so-called psychogeography. We came up with the idea of doing a small project here. Walking – thinking about this city in those terms.'

'What ideas are those?' she asks.

'So there's this guy Robinson, he's like the King of Psychogeography, in the UK at least. He's walked London over and over, mapping and interpreting it in his own way, using poets and myth to understand the soul of the city and how it is reflected in the landscape. That sort of stuff.'

'And you're going to do that here?'

'Kind of, but with added extras.' I reply.

'Go on.' she urges.

'Not now, Mum.' Ben gets out of his chair and turns towards the door.

I smile at her, 'Robinson draws his fans in with references to Blake and the romantics. Our project will be more about outsiders, how a city keeps people down, especially queers – in their place. I, we, want to try out some new methods and then do something about it.'

'So he's still alive then, this Robinson?' she asks.

I nod, 'Though you wouldn't think it sometimes. He's too much of an observer, just sits there hoping something will happen.'

'Well, Ben's got nothing better to do with his time, but what do you do when you're not doing this?'

I pause, I'm not used to saying it, and it has to sound right. I speak as clearly and casual as I can, 'I'm

23

an artist. This is my current practice interest.'

June looks at me, 'You're not from around here are you?' Your accent sounds just like my wife's.'

I feign disinterest and look at my watch.

'Midlands Carpet town was it?' she asks.

I smile.

'Bingo!' She crows.

I've had enough of her for now, picking away. Ben has too, he gets up from his chair, 'Time for our first walk into the city.'

Chapter 6

At the end of his front path, the steep cul-de-sac drops away in front of us – like we're teetering on the end of a diving board, poised above the city.

'So there it is, Ben, the place that pisses you off.'

He flinches as I touch him on the shoulder but I leave my hand there,

'What did Robinson say? 'Regency sandcastles surrounding an ecclesiastical heart of amber, sat in a bowl of English countryside under a wedgewood blue sky.'

I run my hand slowly down his back, letting it come to rest at the top of his ass. He glances around but he doesn't move away.

'Cummon, let's do this.' I say, 'And remember, just walk your usual route.'

As we start in the direction of the city it's clear Ben's feeling self-conscious – I see it in his clumsy walk, suddenly kind of flat footed as if he's trying to act. He sweeps an arm from one side to another. 'It was orchards here before these houses were built, and before, during the Roman period, vineyards.'

I let him burble on while I let my body take in the slope as the landscape pulls us down into the city. The direct nature of the route makes me think that if layers of time were stripped off this landscape, there would be an ancient track beneath our feet.

After 200 metres or so, we cross a steep lane that runs down into the valley, and in what seems like a continuation of the track, we join another street that flattens out and hugs the side of the slope. On our left, a modest Victorian residential terrace, each property with a tiny garden in front. On the right, large garages are joined by long terraced gardens climbing up to older, grander houses on the road above.

'So, you're adopted?' I ask.

'No, my other mum, Mom, she's dead now. She had me - a sperm donation from their friend.'

'Have your family always lived here?'

'Yes, Mum is from around here. But I went to Uni in Manchester, I was there for seven years, I moved back here three years ago.

'How did you find moving back?'

As soon as I say it, Ben's shoulders slump with an already-given-up vibe. The road we're on turns into a small cobbled path which dog-legs up some steps and along the front of a small terrace of cottages.

Your other mum, Mom, she's from Kiddy then, like me?'

'Kidderminster. Yeah, I was born there too.'

This revelation makes me horny. I've never shagged anyone from my hometown - that deep down we belong to the same fields, same paths, somehow belonging. And the thought confuses me, being so contrary to my other feelings about the place. I follow

26

my impulse and decide I don't want to talk about where I've come from. Who I am now is what I am.

At the end of the terrace the path narrows further and zig-zags into an alleyway. 'How do you find your way around? I feel like I'm trespassing.'

Ben snorts in agreement, 'There's lots of this around here, they're not even rights of way, these permissive paths.'

'I get it, and if you think about how we are moving across the landscape, these alleyways are like diversions where the newer buildings have blocked the path.'

'And they're still at it. I was out walking over on the other side of the valley recently, following a clearly marked public footpath on an up-to-date OS map. I came up against a pile of felled trees, and water was being diverted into a hollow in the path to create a bog. There was no way around and I had to turn back.'

'Who are these fuckers?'

'Someone buys a big old house, they don't like walkers on the paths that cross their land and so they take matters into their own hands. Whoever they are, new money or old, that's the pervasive attitude in this city.'

'Entitled bastards.'

We reach a wrought iron fence, behind which a clump of gigantic pines tower over us.

Ben looks up at them, 'They're quite something aren't they? They might even be as old as the Georgian part of the city we're about to enter.'

'They're like from one of those old paintings, landscape scenes of Roman temples, ancient civilization.'

'Yes, a continuing obsession with the classical and picturesque that I've grown to hate, there's no room for anything new.'

I can taste his bile, good, we're getting somewhere.

And so we walk into the picture.

Chapter 7

'Our first Georgian street proper' says Ben. 'Where the artisans would have been, they still are in a way.' He points to a window framed in deep pink.

I stop and look at the window display, huge cakes all white and pastel coloured icing and unicorns, 'It's beyond camp.'

I step closer and press my nose against the glass and peer in. A tall bear of a guy in a white apron stands behind a fussy counter, tying a pink ribbon around a small cake box. 'You ever been in?'

'God no!'

I'm amused by his disgust. 'Not tempted by this rainbow cake?'

'It's been in the window since the place opened, years ago.'

I wink at him as I reach for the door handle. A cute bell tinkles and I pull Ben inside behind me.

The shop is empty of customers except for three posh old ladies sitting at a small table with views up and down the street. They're taking coffee, sharing a salver of profiteroles. The one with a round face uses a dessert spoon to dish a single choux-ball onto each of their plates. I'm sure that she wrinkles her nose as we walk past.

I go up to the counter with Ben. I easily read the bear's guarded but polite look. He might be a queen, but his business interests clearly lie in the service of the old money sitting at the table behind us.

'Yes gentlemen?' says the bear.

I release my best slow smile. 'I love the Pride cake in the window. Do you have a slice to take out?'

'Oh, you mean the rainbow layer. That's a display cake, we can make it to order.'

Now his reply is polite enough, except for the tone, which claims the rainbow concept for My Little Pony princesses and tests out my spending power at the same time.

'You got anything else queer, homosexual if possible?'

The bear glances around the shop, the ladies glance in our direction, smelling excitement. The bear's face hardens, 'What we have for now, is here, right in front of you, gentlemen.'

Ben seems to have become invisible, though he must be right beside me. My fists tighten in my pockets, 'Can you recommend anything for masculine tastes?' I say, letting my eyes slide down the front of the bear's apron.

'Pooves,' in a barely disguised, light and dismissive tone, comes from one of the hags at the profiterole table.

I turn around and look at them. They are facing me down. I almost giggle but just like when someone has found your funny bone, the sharp discomfort finds you first.

I decide on the ringleader, the one that looks like a stick insect, her sharp blue eyes locked onto mine. I walk up to her and bring my face close, our noses almost touch, I smell expensive perfume. She doesn't flinch. She raises her hand and slowly pushes my forehead back with a blotched bony finger. The iciness of her touch penetrates my skull. I hold my ground but she presses harder. I waver, and surprised by my first experience of these creatures, I step back.

She croaks in triumph.

Humiliated, I turn away. I try to act as if nothing happened, casually picking up a glossy local life magazine from a side table as I make for the door.

'Good day to you all.' I call out as the soft bell rings our exit.

Outside, I stumble a few steps as if I've been punched. The uneven slabbed path looks ready to trip me up. I stop to lean against the wall but it refuses to hold me up, it tilts away from me and I topple to the ground.

Ben looks down at me, 'Are you ok?' He reaches out a hand and pulls me up, looking at me wide-eyed, 'That was bonkers! What were you doing in there?'

I stand there, confused, my forehead still cold where she had poked.

'I'm not really sure. It just happened.'

'Well, welcome to my world. You've just encountered one of the grand duchesses that run the place. She's got nerve, I'll give her that.'

Suddenly, I'm struck by the scorching path of one of my lightening blushes, it explodes just below my left ear and shoots across my face up to my right temple. I wrench my fists from my pockets and punch the honeyed stone wall several times with both fists.

It helps.

Ben tries to comfort me, 'The oldies are the worst.'

'I don't care about those fucking harpies.'

Ben's underestimating me. I'm going to use the experience to power up.

Chapter 8

As we pass a small flea market, no doubt peddling tat from the grand houses, I sense an opportunity, 'Your Riku, he liked places like this didn't he?'

'He came to this one a lot.'

But that's all he says and I want to know more, 'Are you still in touch?'

'Not much since the artbook was made.'

I see his heart in his face – he'd been head over heels for this guy. I dig, 'How many copies were made?'

'Only Five. Handmade in Japan using traditional methods.'

'Rare then?'

'I suppose.' His gaze drifts to nowhere, his mind has floated back to Riku.

The dark heart, the Abbey, comes into full view.

"Isn't it too small to be a city?' I ask.

'If it wasn't for the historical religious connections, you're right.'

Here in the old city I find my back starting to ache and I'm feeling narky. We pass close to a queue of tourists waiting outside a tiny shop front, a period tea house specialising in the local bun.

'What was here before the Georgian? A lot

of the old mediaeval city which would have been around here was ripped out during the 1960s urban modernisation plan. The 'good people' called it 'The Sack of the City'.'

'The 'good people'?'

'It's a term Mum uses ironically. She means those upper middle classes, whose opinions dominate the city. They focus on conserving everything as it is, appropriating heritage to strengthen their own position.'

We arrive in a small square lined by The Pump Rooms, The Roman Baths and the Abbey, whose deafening bells are clanging. Locals swirl past slower moving tourists.

'It's like Soho really.' I say. 'This city trades on its past, Roman Baths and impressive Georgian architecture. In Soho's case it's all mid twentieth century post-war sleaze.'

'I hadn't thought of it like that.'

'Soho flavour is go-go girl shows, film and music industry offices, Ronnie Scott's, the swinging 60s, gay bars, Bar Italia, prostitution, a whiff of the Krays. But that's beside the point, how often do you have to come into this hellhole?'

'A lot, small food shopping, picking up books from the library, getting Mum's prescriptions from the chemist.'

I'm feeling overwhelmed and feel the need to break out.

Chapter 9

My hopes of escape are slim as this cultural theme park just keeps on giving. Outside the Jane Austen Centre an old man in period costume, his port red cheeks perfect for the role, poses for photos with tourists. He stands proud next to a life-size dummy of the iconic novelist, she looks as bored as I feel.

We're in heritage overload territory when we reach a four storey circular terrace of Georgian townhouses around a green dominated by huge fuck off plane trees which must have been planted when the place was built.

Ben gestures towards a guy riding a long sit-up-and-beg bike with a delivery-box up front with 'Yes Sir!' painted across it in gold lettering.

'Watch this.' says Ben.

The rider slows to a stop. He's middle-aged, dragged up in period breeches. As he steps off his bike it's clear that he's really tall. He opens the carriage box and takes out a single white envelope.

'Is he for real?' I ask.

'Yes sir, Yes sir, three bags full sir! It'll be some birthday card or an invitation to some high society event.'

Lanky steps across to a front door of one of the

circus properties, presses the highly polished brass doorbell and takes a step back. Some old Dame answers. Lanky holds out the card in one hand and makes a low bow. She takes the card, smiles thinly and smartly closes the door.

'What the fuck? Who are these people?' I ask.

'That, my dear man, is one of the 'good people' of the City. No doubt friends of those ladies you encountered in the patisserie.'

I feel a bubbling anger in my chest but I'm resolved to just watch today, take things in. I follow Ben as he heads for the shade of the trees.

We sit down on the grass. I get my near empty pack of cigarettes out, 'How come you ended up here?'

Ben thinks and when he finally speaks he struggles to get his words out, 'Well, I was at Uni, the phd, but it drifted, went wrong. Then money got a bit tight and it seemed like the easy option.'

'Do you have any mates here?'

'Well. Writers group mainly, but then they scurry back off to their lives.'

'Any gays , friends with benefits at least?'

'I see a few couples around. same thing though.'

'Heteronormativity rules around here I reckon – gays trying blend in.'

I look at him, almost lifeless as a result of being stuck here – he's hollowed out, poor sod. I light up and scan the posh terrace, 'Look at how this place reflects its corruption.'

'Maybe for those that live here in The Circus, but

most of the people in the city are not so rich. They just put on the airs and graces.'

'Are you defending them? What they do is worse, accepting the 'good people' as their role models whilst at the same time doffing their caps. They're trapped in the idea that this is the right way to live, fucking zombies.'

Ben looks at me, hurt, as I drag deep on my ciggy.

'I'm not trying to defend them, just provide some facts.'

I soften my tone, 'I remember a line from a Samuel R Delaney novel I read once. I can't remember which one, 'How should people rebel and modernise a city that wont change?'

Ben gazes into the distance as if he's trying to find an answer then and there. I take another drag and blow a smoke ring in his direction.

'Tomorrow it's my turn. We'll drift, a classic Debord derive.'

He smiles and lies back in the grass. 'Tell me more about Robinson.'

I sneer, 'Oh so he exists for you now then?'

'Cummon. Tell me about you and him.'

I look at him, 'Have you watched the Keiller films yet?'

'I haven't.'

'Something to look forward to then. He's like how he's portrayed, especially in the first one. Except that he's a dirty old fucker. But he knows his stuff, he should be more influential really.'

'He sounds interesting.'

'He knows about this project.'

Ben's face brightens, 'What? Does he know about me?'

'Do you want him to know about you?'

'Well yes I suppose.'

I laugh, 'Be careful what you wish for.' I stub my cigarette out in the grass and spring to my feet. 'I'll see what I can do, puppy, but now I've got to go. Till tomorrow.'

He looks bewildered but I give him no chance to protest. I'm gone already.

Chapter 10

On the heat, I stir stolen oats into gold top milk, hoping a comfort breakfast might soothe my dark mood.

Zach, the hostel manager is hovering – he's cute but too straight laced – probably from a youth misspent in the Boy Scouts. It's past 10am and I should be out of here. From his lack of eye contact I think he's weighing up how difficult I might be.

I stare at the porridge in the worn out pan, frowning at the thought of Ben's pitiful attitude yesterday. But it's the Duchess from the cake shop that's put me in this mood, she really caught me on the hop.

I turn breakfast out into a bowl and take it over to one of the tables. As I eat, my superfood does its work and my determination builds. What happened yesterday is not going to happen again. Nobody else in this city is going to do that to me.

As I eat, I use my phone to check my hair. There's no need for the Cliff Richard bouffant anymore, I've left that version of myself behind. Now my hair hangs naturally, thick strands drape over my eyes, Riku style. It's not dark like his must be, but it should do the trick on Ben. I set my camera to monochrome, ramp up the exposure, look seriously at the camera and video myself.

'Konichiwa. Konichiwa, watashi wa Manny desu.'

I play-back several times. Yes, cool.

But it's a weak dopamine hit and I feel the breath seeping out of my chest. My head drops and a wave of sadness, regret and self doubt presses down on my shoulders. It's not about Riku, it's about what happened in Soho. It went too far between me and Jimmy Dean.

When I'd told Robinson about it, he said that I shouldn't have objectified him, that I should have been more professional. I pushed back, saying that was the whole point – that we were objectifying each other – both role playing – there was no pulling out half way through. Robinson had then waffled on about blurred lines between art and reality. He's worse than useless sometimes.

Truth is though, I hadn't told Robinson everything I'd 'read' when I'd run my hands over Jimmy Dean's body, I'd just alluded to the sensations. I wouldn't have been able to explain properly and he wouldn't have believed me anyway. Also, even though we've had sex loads of times, Robinson and me, and though I really wanted to, I've never scan-tripped him. Partly because I'd set myself up as his passive plaything. But I'd also been too scared of being caught in the act – and of what I might read.

I sigh to myself – Robinsons criticisms or not, my self-doubt or not, it's time to look forward and focus on this project and get my ass over to Ben's.

Chapter 11

I'm in no mood for his Mum today – I message Ben to meet me on the street above theirs. Whilst I wait, I check my bank balance on my phone - it's worryingly low but at the same time I find it exciting. It's always been like this with me, it's a kind of turn on. But I also recognise I need to take care, I don't want to be distracted back into hustling right now.

Ben comes out of the house, there's a spring in his step and he's shaping his hair with his hand as he walks. He's into me for sure. When he appears at the top of the steps, I see he's clean shaven, he's really made an effort. His eyes take in my floppy hair and they can't resist coming back for more, like a kid licking an ice cream.

'Morning, Manny. You should've come in, Mum's taken a shine to you.'

I pull a 'torn' face.

'So it's a Dérive today?' he asks.

'Yes, you ready for some disorientanteering?'

I've decided to head uphill, turning randomly into a lane before forking off onto a steep path through a strip of woodland.

Ben's talkative, 'It still feels surreal. We chat on a website. And now.' His voice sounds romantic.

'And now, I'm leading you astray just behind your house.'

Ben dismisses me with a more serious look, 'I know you said all that clever stuff to Mum yesterday but what exactly are you here for, it can't just be exploring my boredom with this place?'

'Be patient.'

'Do you have any other projects on the go? And I never asked, but what do you do for a living?'

'I manage, I travel light. That London project paid.'

He glances across at me.

I laugh. 'Ha! I'm doing this for the love of it, unless you want to pay me?'

His look is still so serious.

'I'm joking.' I add.

Ben softens, 'It's great you're here. I'm trying to write about it.'

I don't tell him about the notes and stuff I'm keeping about him, 'I was gonna ask, other than Chronostasis, have you had anything else published?'

'A nonfiction piece in Litro – about a trip I did in Northern Greece. Why? Are you going to check it out? It's not very good, I think my style has moved on.'

'Don't put yourself down, you're published, people will have read your work, some will have thought about what you wrote. That's something.'

As we come out of the woods the distant view is dominated by a treeless hill with a broad plateau. It makes me think of a pudding turned out of a bowl.

Ben notices my interest, 'Solsbury Hill, you know, from the Peter Gabriel song?'

'I don't know it.'

I stop to take it in. It stands out different, as if shaped by another geology, lighter green to the countryside around it.

We turn away and join a small lane, continuing our rise. After a short steep climb, our way levels out into a large triangular green with a children's playground in the centre.

A few lingering toddlers are being watched by sitting and standing women. One of the benches near the climbing frame is free and I make a beeline for it, fumbling in my pockets for my cigarettes. As we sit down a few of the women gaze our way.

'They're checking us out aren't they? As if we're possible paedo's.' I ask, rolling my eyes.

'Oh I don't know.'

In fairness, a couple of them haven't batted an eyelid, they seem friendly even, but the overall atmosphere is suspicion and low level hostility.

I light up and gaze in their direction, considering them. Sure, they're exercising their parental instincts, but there's another layer to their disapproval, as if we're somewhere we shouldn't be and not just because of the kids.

I blow a circle of smoke out in the direction of two mums giving instructions to their offspring in voices loud enough to be heard for miles.

'I'm not sure what I think about breeders.' I say.

Ben looks shocked. 'You seem in a bad mood today'

'They piss me off, throwing their weight around. Like the world belongs to them and they're doing us all a favour by having kids.'

'Women?'

'Straights.' I look away, trying to ignore them, 'I thought we'd get a view of the city from up here.'

Ben smiles, 'Depends which way you drift.'

I stand up and get my phone out. 'Come on, I need you.'

I go over to the kids roundabout. It has a steel bar frame shaped like a traffic cone. I boss him. 'Go on, get on and face me. No not like that, splay yourself like da Vinci man.'

A couple of tots wander closer, happily gurgling. I take Ben's photo; but as he goes to get off, I step towards him.

'No, wait.' I grab the iron frame and pull to my left. It begins to turn.

A mum comes across and attempts to usher the toddlers away from us, but they appear to be caught in two minds.

Ben laughs as I spin him faster, he's having to grip hard.

'Manny! Enough!'

The kids are squealing in delight. I video the scene.

'Manny!'

He looks nauseous and about to lose his grip. I pretend to show mercy, using both arms to grab onto a bar and bring the roundabout to a juddering stop. I step forward and press his shoulders back against the frame and lean into him, 'Not done yet sexy boy. You gotta go the other way now.'

'Oh no, please!'

'Come on, it's fun, do it for me.'

I kiss him lightly on the lips. He looks over my shoulder for a second, then he submits.

'Hold on, Ben.'

I start to spin him the other way. He groans. The adults lead their 'little ones' away, packing up and heading off, amidst the children's pleas, tears and mounting tantrums.

Meanwhile I imagine Ben is in some sort of generator and I'm spinning energy into him, charging him up.

When I've finished with him, Ben steps off, staggers around and drops down onto the grass. I sit down next to him and touch his leg.

He twitches it away, 'What was all that about?'

I say nothing. I'd just wanted to quieten my anger by exercising a bit of power and control.

We sit in silence for a few minutes.

I take out the now crumpled packet of Lucky Strike's and my lighter.

Ben is grumpy, 'I didn't think people really smoked anymore, isn't it really expensive?'

'I don't really smoke. It was part of the last project,

part of my look.' I flick out the remaining cigarette and light up.

Maybe because it's the last one from that packet, from that night, but I'm thinking about my Jimmy Dean. I cringe at what he'd begged me to do with the smouldering cigarette tip – and it triggers the smell of singed flesh. I throw the fag on the grass and stub it out.

I roll onto my front and sniff the grass in the hope of clearing the memory from my nostrils. I see Ben out of the corner of my eye, staring at me.

I push my nose in deeper so that it presses into the dampness of the soil below the surface. I breathe it in, and press my body against the green, closing my eyes. My body senses the tilt of the hill and for a moment I'm inside it, like an astronaut on a space-walk on the dark side of the moon. I want to know how deep below the surface this straight dominated landscape goes. I have no idea how to reach an answer.

Chapter 12

We leave the green and the path I choose drops towards the city – it's not long before we're walking through a large ornamental park. A summer shower catches us in shirtsleeves and we look around for cover. Ben points towards a footpath, 'Go that way, we're close to the Artists Studios. My friend, Geoff, works there. If he's in we might get a coffee. I'll text him.'

We start jogging as the rain pelts down.

'I didn't think you had any friends here?' I shout.

'I know him from Uni. He lives over in Wiltshire.'

'Artist studios' sounds cool.'

'Don't get excited, it's mostly well-off old hippies with time and money to spare. Geoff is cool though.'

The shower stops as we exit the park. We cross a main road and slip into a large yard set behind an old warehouse. A small art gallery is joined to what looks like an old workshops building, they must be the studios. A lean-to provides cover for an old table and two white plastic chairs. The ashtray on the table is full with roll-up stubs.

Ben leads us to a battered door next to the gallery entrance. We peer briefly through the wired glass window before Ben presses the buzzer. A skinny poker-faced woman springs out of what looks like a store-room and glares at us through the glass whilst reaching for the latch. She opens the door just wide enough to frame her hostile face. She looks at me, dismisses me out of hand and focuses on Ben, waiting.

Ben is polite, 'We're here to see Geoff. He said he'll be down in a mo.'

'You should wait, just over there.' she says pointing to the lean-to.

'Oh, he said to wait in the Common Room.'

She sniffs, 'Oh he did? That's not really for guests. Well, you better come in, I suppose.'

A few steps down the corridor she stops and points to a door, 'In there.' before nudging past us and skitting back into her den.

We're greeted by a kitchen sink and a worktop stained with tea and scattered with stray coffee crystals. A grimy kettle completes the look. The room opens out – four identical cheap blue sofas are grouped around a low coffee table littered with magazines and fliers. Along one wall, large windows face through the lean-to and out into the yard.

Each sofa has been claimed. Three by almost identical, older women in smocks and aprons smeared with dried paint and clay. A muscular guy sits on the remaining sofa, head bent over his hands as he rolls a cigarette.

The stockiest of the women points a stuffed pitta in our direction, 'Are you here for a class? Are you lost?' in a deep and accusing tone.

I smile, 'If this is the common room then we're in

the right place.'

I plonk myself down next to her, on her sofa, opposite Smoker Boy. The women conjure a collective silent huff before resuming a conversation that seems to be about 'the staff'. Ben remains standing, he picks up a dog eared copy of the city society magazine from the coffee table and starts flicking through it.

'Arran' clips the woman next to me. 'You're with us on this aren't you?'

He nods without looking up. 'Of course, Angie.'

The movement of his hands looks familiar. He looks up and a stab of recognition shoots through my body followed by feelings of worthlessness and hot shame, then cold anger. So he's called Arran is he? He seems to notice me too but only for a split second.

Arran's broad face and high cheekbones have perfect dimensions but he's not what you'd call beautiful. He's attractive in a nasty way, one that promises sketchiness. He looks extra hot in that paint-splattered trackie top, thin non-matching jogging bottoms and battered Doc Marten boots.

He stands up, unlit ciggy in the corner of his mouth whilst he takes out a box of swan vestas from a pocket.

He looks across at me, 'Hey. Have we met before?' he drawls.

His voice sounds posher than when I last talked with him. I let my hair drop further over my eyes and shake my head, 'Don't think so, mate.'

'Central St Martins?'

So he remembers. I shake my head and throw out a decoy. 'I got friends in a studio in Manchester, you know Angel Mill?'

Arran makes a derisive scoff, 'Nah, never been to Manchester, not that far North.' and with that he turns and walks out of the door.

He reappears seconds later, visible through the window, lighting up under the shelter, glancing in my direction from time to time. Towards the end of his ciggy he catches my eye with more purpose and starts walking along the front of the building before I lose sight of him.

Another guy walks into the common room – he might be tall if his posture wasn't so stooped. He's wearing a frayed fisherman's sweater and he's got a craggy, weather blasted face to go with it.

'Hi Ben.'

Ben smiles and walks towards him.

Geoff looks a fair bit older than us, forties, fifties, and I wonder about the precise details of how they met.

'What brings you here?' Geoff asks whilst stepping forward with open arms towards Ben. Geoff emits a little squawk like laugh as they gently hug.

'We got caught by the rain and seeing as we were close by.'

They step back from each other and Geoff looks in my direction.

'This is Manny,' says Ben, 'We're doing a project, like, to err, explore certain aspects of the city. There's a lot of walking involved.'

Geoff nods appreciatively as he goes over to the kitchenette, fills the gross kettle from the tap and looks across at me,'Would you like a Tea or Coffee, Ben?'

'Black coffee please. Sorry, but where's the toilet?'

Geoff points to the other end of the room, 'Through that door and straight ahead.'

I'm outside the mens toilets. I know something's going to happen, just from the way my body feels, that fizzing adrenalin, the nice sort - intoxicating my brain, livening my balls. My hand feels jittery as I push on the door and go in.

Arran's there, smirking, leaning against the wall next to a shelf piled with green paper hand towels. I take in the rest of the space, two empty cubicles and a urinal. I feel horny and angry at the same time, a dangerous cocktail where I'm concerned.

'It was you then?' he asks.

'When did you acquire the posh voice or did you always have it?

He tilts his head dismissively, 'What brings you here then?'

I glance at the urinal, 'Not you.'

He laughs quietly, 'Yeah, but now I'm here, right here in front of you, I think I know what you want.' He arches his back and slowly pushes out his hips.

'Don't be so sure. Anyway, more to the point - what are you doing here?'

'I'm from around here, my studio is here, but fuck that, cummon, what about now?' He slides his hand inside the waistband of his trackie bottoms and takes a step closer.

I feel a blush strike across my face. Yes, I owe him!

He chuckles, 'Aww, he's blushing. Cute. I didn't have you down as the sensitive type.'

I'd seen Arran around the art-student circuit in London, I'd come onto him a couple of times. Eye contact, that sort of stuff. He'd teased me, and some. Then, late one night, we bumped into each other in the street. I was walking back from a night out - him the same no doubt. I wanted to be his friend, he wanted something else. He pissed on me then had me suck him off, right there in that alleyway.

A couple of weeks later, when I spotted him in a bar, I made the mistake of approaching him to say hello. As I got within speaking distance he turned away and shared some private joke with the girl and boy he was with.

This situation now is damned hot, but I'm not forgiving humiliations like that.

I take a step towards him – we're within touching distance of each other. I reach out a hand towards his crotch and let it hover midair, waiting for his permission. He removes his hand from his tracksuit, sniffs it and nods. I grab his hard cock through the polyester and use it to pull him to me. We kiss with building aggression, our mouths playing out a battle for supremacy. I let him take control, for now.

Breaking our kiss, I rush to unzip his trackie top and roughly push my hands up under his t-shirt, I feel the power in my hands as they pause on his back just below his shoulders. I tell myself that I don't have enough time, but my hands ignore my warning and run up across his smooth back, coming together, pressing hard at his neck before slowly feeling their way down his spine, my eyeballs flickering behind shut eyelids, my hands magnetised to his strong torso.

My scan-trip is fleeting - oak panelling – a crest – the smell of school. Power plays - bigger boys dominate younger ones physically but don't get it all their own way mentally.

The vision is broken as he grabs my face and aggressively forces his tongue into my mouth. He doesn't know what he's playing with. He's just another one of those posh boys of the city, dragged up as an artist. This is his city, those potters back there, these are his people. He'll end up burdened with a wife, kids and au-pair grazing up on the green.

But for now here he is, with his tongue deep in my mouth. He's taller than me and pressing down on me. I know we're on an edge. He doesn't. I'm feeling lost in his mouth, my hands still in awe of the beef of his body. He slides his hands under the back of my jeans and pulls on my pants hard, as if to choke my ass. I'm tempted to let him win. My tongue pushes forward and deep in his mouth I get a hint of sugary chocolate sweetness.

His forehead is pressing down on me, concentrated on one point, the very point where that old woman's finger in the cake shop had pushed me back. I feel the rage race across my face again and as his tongue pushes back deep into my mouth I bite hard. I taste the metallic as he yanks himself away, blood already running across his lips.

'You crazy fuck. What are you doing?' he shouts as he lunges towards me.

I push him back against the wall, he's no match – I have a purpose – he's confused.

I turn away and look into the mirror, my deep blush still there, like my face has been brushed by a thunderbolt. I've never seen it this deep and I take a quick photo of myself in the mirror, him in the background holding his bleeding mouth. He's too shocked to retaliate. I turn around to face him and raise my eyebrows with a smirk glancing in the direction of the common room to remind him where he is,

'Let's put it this way – if you don't know why then you're even more of a twat than I thought you were.'

Of course, it's not about that but he doesn't deserve an explanation.

I push him out of the way and go back into the common room.

Chapter 13

We leave the studios the back way – out onto the riverside path. Ben can't wait to get stuck into me, 'What was all that about?' You went to the toilet and came back all different, and with blood on your lips – I heard raised voices, was that Arran?'

I'm liking the vein of jealousy I sense in his questions.

'Turns out we knew each other. I had a score to settle. He's part of the problem anyway.'

'God – I hope it doesn't get back to Geoff.'

As we walk back into town, the brown river flows past us in the opposite direction – given up on trying to be scenic. I feel like we're getting behind the facade of this place. Behind the railway station, Victorian civil engineering dominates – buddleia and perennial weeds are well established – the path is strewn with empty plastic bottles and snack wrappers - a bugged out monkey artwork sprayed onto the side of a small electrical substation. Ben is going on about some red brick housing but I'm stuck in my head trying to figure out what to do to make my project a success. I see the divisions in the people and the landscape, how the 'good people' control everything – the layout of the city, the design of the houses, the public spaces.

The likes of me might move differently through these spaces but the archaeology is theirs. Plus, I need to prove myself to Robinson. There's no going back anyway, I've got nowhere to go back to.

And Ben – and what does he think of me? I think back to the first night we chatted online. I'd come home pissed and dejected again from a party at Goldsmiths. Ben had been drinking too, in his bedroom, a hundred miles away. It was that night we dreamt up this project. He said his writing was stuck, he felt boxed in, never getting beyond the first draft of a story about his isolation in the city. I'd regurgitated what Robinson had fed to me about the outsider and the city. I didn't tell Ben that I just needed to keep moving, that's how I stayed alive. And so here I am, here we are, walking, walking. But for all my doubts he's with me, walking close to me, like he wants to touch me. On the other hand things haven't moved on, I've got work to do, I need to turn up the heat.

As I come back out of my reverie, I see he's staring at my red trainers.

'Like them?' I ask.

He nods appreciatively.

We pass under a damp and dripping industrial bridge before the river bends once more, this time opening up a view of a weir and an older bridge topped with a row of Georgian buildings.

'The city's version of the Ponte Vecchio, in Florence.' says Ben.

I'm not interested, I've seen a hangar curved roof

just beyond a grassed rampart worn with shortcuts to concrete stairs leading up onto a glass entrance of a leisure centre. I point to a bench facing the river, 'Wait here a minute.'

Five minutes later, I waft two tickets in front of his face, 'We're in luck, they have a sauna, it is a spa town after all. Cummon, this is where you can really find out about a place.'

He groans, 'But we don't have trunks and stuff.'

'We can work around that. I've even hired a towel, my treat.'

'One towel?'

'You get first dibs. Promise.'

Ben pulls a face and reluctantly gets to his feet.

I point down at the worn dusty track in the grass rampart, 'These shortcuts are called 'lines of desire', they show everyday comings and goings as people deviate from the paths they are supposed to follow.'

'Really.' Ben replies with little interest.

'It's an important concept of queer theory, especially when looking for the visual evidence of our presence in the landscape.'

He ignores me. Seems like he can't wait to get this over and done with.

I reject the unisex Changing Village in favour of one of two male communal changing rooms in the back corridor. I study Ben's body as we strip down to

57

our underwear. His boxers are baggy and a shyness has him half turned away from me. He's hairier than I thought, with a denseness that covers even his shoulders and lower back. I imagine how it feels to brush against that extra layer of pleasure, body to body.

I'm smooth except for my pubes and a tiny amount of armpit hair. My hips are curvier than I'd like but they drive some guys wild. I'm wearing the classic Wolsey y-fronts from the Soho project which artist Roy thought I looked so good in that he let me keep them.

I insist on separate lockers. I've thought this through. I tell him it's because everything I've brought from London is in that backpack.

I shower opposite Ben so that he sees the warm water splash down my body and transform my y-fronts from clean white to shady translucent, the cotton clinging to my cock.

The spa is a joke – a small plunge pool, one shower and a tiny sauna cabin. When we take the last two spaces in the cabin, our arrival is acknowledged by nods, a breath, small leg movements. I take the higher bench and ease in between a wrinkly old guy and an athletic younger woman. Ben perches down in the corner by the thermometer.

There's a guy sitting opposite Ben, short, smooth and super fit, with small jug handle ears, a diamante stud in each. Light blue shorts cling to his smooth thighs. He will bring things to the boil nicely if I play it right. I don't want to take my eyes off him but my attention would be counterproductive.

So when Diamond Boy looks up at me, I close my eyes and focus on the heat and the sweat pushing its way out of my body.

When I open my eyes, Diamond Boy has switched his attention to Ben but he seems oblivious, even when during some cabin conversation Diamond says he's here twice a week whilst looking directly at Ben!

Time to take it up a gear, 'Cummon Ben, plunge pool.'

We climb the three steps and stand there looking down into the blue cube. I step off and drop in with a loud splash. A freezing rush from pain to ecstasy in under a second as the neural messages shoot up my spine to my brain's cortex before the water reaches my neck.

Ben takes the ladder and slowly lowers himself in before letting himself submerge.

He resurfaces with a laugh, 'Fuck, amazing!' His voice echoes around the room.

I edge closer and gently elbow him, 'You've got a friend.' I say in a low, quiet voice.

Ben's dismissive. He's clueless - I'm gonna have to do the work.

'Anyway, what do you think of this place?' I ask.

'It's good. I can't quite work out what it is I like.'

'People talking on the level to each other?'

'And the accents are different.'

I lean across and speak into his ear, 'No sign of

59

those entitled bastards. It gives me hope that another city exists besides the shit I've come up against so far.'

I edge towards the ladder, ready to get out, 'Ben, no questions, stay here another minute at least.'

As I reach the sauna door, Diamond Boy comes out, and holds the door for me, all the time with his eyes on Ben. Good, at least he got the message.

Diamond Boy showers in clear view of Ben - the pin-like jets of water bouncing off his taut skin. He turns slowly like a cake on a revolving stand waiting to be iced. His self ease is beautiful and it matches the open honesty of his conversation. He knows himself and he knows the world around him. I like that.

Diamond Boy drops into the pool without a single splash. Seconds later I hear him and Ben talking and looking at their body language, this is going to plan. Their 'mating ritual' cycle of sauna, plunge, shower goes on for another 20 minutes.

When Ben decides to call it a day and head to the changing room, Diamond Boy follows. I leave it a couple of minutes before I do the same.

When I get to the changing room I hear voices, just theirs. I quietly retrieve my backpack and slip into the changing room next door. There's no showers in here but there is an adjoining door. I put my ear to the cool wood.

'What do you do?' asks Diamond Boy.

'Err I write, do workshops now and then. You?'.

'Oh, a clever one. I'm a bricklayer, working for my dad. We're renovating a posh house just outside town at the moment.'

I hear the showers, more muffled conversation. One shower stops, then another - then the rub of towels.

'I got a half day today – just finished a gym session,' says Diamond Boy. 'You do sport or something, you look like you might.'

This is hotting up.

'Just hiking. You?'

'Boxing, Amateur like. I trained with England last year though.'

I grab my phone from my bag and hold the camera lens against the keyhole, taking shots and video. Diamond Boy naked, towel only half covering his cock, Ben with our towel over his lap sat on a bench, they're within touching distance of each other.

I'm hard now. I crouch down and peer through the keyhole.

'Did you ever play footy?' asks Diamond Boy. 'You've got the legs for it.'

'Err, thanks.' Ben says nervously, clearly unsure of how to treat this newfound attention.

OK , hot enough. Time to interrupt.

I'm saved the trouble by Diamond Boy's mobile's 'Call me when you want, call me when you need.' ringtone.

Diamond boy drops his towel and picks up his phone. 'Hi. I'm at the leisure centre. Yeah, just about finished. When? 5 mins!? Ok. Ok. I'll be there.'

Diamond Boy curses under his breath – dressing

rapidly and stuffing his gear into a sports bag.

'Dad's picking me up! I can't keep him waiting. See you here again? Tuesdays and Thursdays I'm here, about this time. I'm Sol.'

'Ben.'

'Catch ya later, Ben.'

The hell you will.

And he was gone.

Job done.

Ben's such a romantic he'll be walking on air all the way home but he'll be ready.

I push open the door, walk in and point at the bench, 'Throw me that towel you cock teaser!'

Chapter 14

June answers the door, she looks as if she's been expecting me. I hold up a package, ready to conjure up a pretext but she waves it away.

I put a finger to my lips and whisper, 'I hope he's not home yet, I need it to be a surprise.'

She stands aside, 'His room's straight across from you at the top of the stairs.'

I'm halfway up, trainers in hand, when she calls up, 'How long are staying in the city, for?'

I turn around, 'I don't know.'

'Where's home?' Her voice is softer now.

'That's complicated.'

'Well, at least he's not moping around – that's changed for the better since you rolled up.'

In Ben's room there's a faint whiff of his biscuityness. A double bed is neatly made up, there's a desk near the window. Framed pictures – a couple of abstract landscapes plus a handful of male portraits, hang on white walls. I check my watch, I should have time to do what I want to do.

His bookshelves are organised. – one for travel guides, one for arty reference books, ones for literature from Japan and Morocco – and on the middle shelf, psychogeography titles, which all look new. I scan them: Coverley, Solnit, Breton, Aragon, Delaney. I've read them, and more, I'm still ahead of the game.

I go to the window and look out over the back garden. Beyond King Apple the neighbouring roofs zig-zag down to the London road. On the other side of the valley, meadows until the thin lines of light reflect off the river, the railway and the canal.

I drop my backpack onto the floor and flop onto the bed. Gazing up at the ceiling, I wonder if this is going to work. It should be a cinch but maybe because he's so likeable, I don't feel certain. I notice a high shelf above the desk, stacked with photo albums, DVDs gathering dust and a metallic mesh box full of notebooks. There might work.

I hear the front door open and freeze.

'Mum, I'm home.'

I hear them talking directly below me – they must be in the kitchen – the conversation sounds domestic, she must be keeping her promise not to spoil the surprise.

I sit up onto the edge of the bed, grab my backpack, and take out the small black felt pouch containing the tiny spycam. Roy had used ones like this to record my activity around the Cube – the results were impressive. I liked that it could be controlled from a mobile phone. I set it up on the shelf, next to the DVDs, giving a view of the desk and bed. It's hardly noticeable. I'm not sure if I even need the footage or how I will explain it to him, I just know I want it and

I'll find a way to explain it to him later, maybe.

I continue browsing his bookshelves and recognise The Rings of Saturn by WG Sebald. I've not read his stuff but Robinson has a thing about 'Max' Sebald, seems to know him, but won't talk about him. I take out the book, go and sit on the desk and start reading the blurb on the back and then I hear footsteps on the stairs. It must be Ben, June would sound more ponderous than that. I fumble for my phone and set the spycam to record. I adjust my hair, run a finger over my bruised lip, and push my ass back on the desk so that my feet dangle off the floor.

Ben enters, not looking anywhere in particular, and like it always is in these situations, a sixth sense kicks in and he jumps back with a loud yelp,

'Bloody hell, Manny!'

I squint at him through the hair flopping over my eyes.

'What are you doing here?' he demands.

I put the book down and smile slowly, slide my right hand into my pocket, leaving my index finger out so it points down into my crotch, like a symbolic gesture from a renaissance portrait. I'd once taken a photo of a guy who'd used this gesture and I knew the effect.

Ben's eyes slyly flicker between mine and the gesture, his breathing shallows. Yep, you're all mine now, Ben, this is what all the sexual tension has been for. I can almost see the sexual energy coursing through him, like liquid mercury, fuelled by Diamond

Boy and about to be ignited by me. Now I'm cashing in, it's for the project.

I ease off the desk and into his personal space. He blinks, as if he senses the danger. I feel his heat on my face, that sweet breath swirling up my nostrils. I close in, so close that I notice, for the first time, tiny freckles scattered across the skin on his cheekbones. I want his mouth now but I hold back and look into his eyes – eyes that are asking, Now? Is it going to happen right now?

I inch a little closer, not touching him, 'Yep.'

Mouth on mouth – my lips slide across his – his body snaps onto mine like iron to lodestone. I deepen the kiss but I don't want him melting, I want him on fire. I pull my face back from his and use my hands to twist on his shoulders and push his face down toward the desk, he shoves his Mac and notebooks out of the way then grabs the edge of the desk with his hands to steady himself. I touch his ass and he automatically pushes it out. I reach around, undo his belt with one hand and yank at his jeans and pants until they slide down his hairy legs and gather around his ankles.

I lean forward and whisper in his ear. 'Yes?'

He tries to look back at me, 'I, err.'

I hesitate, am I just using sex again to get what I want? But I've undone the buttons on my fly and I know it's way too late. I touch his ass with the wet tip of my cock, 'Yes?' I say, more insistent.

His 'Yes' matches my intensity. I scrabble for a condom and lube from my bag, I don't want him freaking out after. I glance up at the shelf in the corner of the room, yes, Robinson's going to love this. I'm distant of course – I watch dispassionately as my fly buttons leave little imprints on his ass cheeks. I don't know why but I hold back from running my hands over his body, this time.

As I thrust into him I'm weighing up what I want the after effect on him to be and what exactly I need to do now to achieve that - will I want him to be my pup, my slave, my lover, or a clueless bimbo. It's a fine line.

When I take myself out and remove the condom, he's flopped out on the desk breathing hard, his legs still shaking. I do myself up and step back.

'Wow. It's been a while. A long while.' Ben says.

I can't resist, 'Riku?'

'No, we didn't.... just some random guy last year.' he says ruefully, pulling his trousers up and starting to tidy the desk, 'I think I should take a shower.'

I grab his hand and pull him onto the bed with me.

He laughs, 'Can we open a window at least? It smells like.'

'No way.'

Chapter 15

          I roll onto one elbow to face Ben, 'Our project. I think it's going to work.'

'Because we just had sex?'

'Partly. I'm serious. I think the body has a connection with the landscape. I'm still working things out but, well sex helps me read the connection. Bodies are important business, beautiful ones especially, because they don't last forever.'

'Is this your spin on psychogeography?'

'Yeah - I got a word I like that describes it, queerscapes.

And I sit up and reach for my backpack, 'Anyway, look at this.'

I take out a large manilla envelope and pass it to him. 'Whilst you were wandering around town dreaming of Diamond Boy, I went to the County Records Office.'

Ben opens it – photocopies of old photographs and postcards of the city.

'Where's this I wonder?' he says, pointing to an image of mediaeval half-timbered buildings.

'That's just it, these are places in the city that are no longer there.'

'Like in that book The Sack Of the Old City?'

'Yes but without the fuckwit conservative

opinions.'

He looks at me, nonplussed.

I tap them, 'These photos give us hope. That change does happen – even here.'

'Perhaps, but it's a World Heritage City now.'

I dismiss his negativity with a shrug.

'I also got this whilst I was there.' I delve back into my bag and pull out a small hardback book.

He holds it in both hands and reads aloud, 'Solsbury Hill, its history and romance.'

'It took all my powers of persuasion to get this loaned out to me.'

Ben studies the cover, 'I like the woodcut depicting the hill, very 1930s. But what's the attraction with Solsbury Hill? It's kind of outside the city.'

I recline back onto the pillows, 'I'm drawn to it. I think I saw it even before I arrived, from the other side. Let's have a walk up there, one day soon.'

'Sure.'

Ben looks at his watch, 'I better go and start making Mum's dinner.'

Fearing the moment is going to drift away, I reach out and stroke his hair, 'Ben, I want what we just did – to mean something.'

He melts back towards me, 'It does, you know it does.'

'For me.' I pause, 'I need to spend the night with you, tonight, here, in your bed. Then it will mean something.'

He looks pleased with himself, he doesn't need to

think twice about what I'm asking,

'Wait here, I'll go and make us all a drink and talk with Mum.'

As I hear his feet on the stairs I pick up my phone from the bedside table and stop the video recording.

Chapter 16

The light's warmth on my eyelids wakes me up and I blink my way into the new day. I'm hanging off Ben's shoulder, curled up, hot and sticky, my thigh clinging to his hip. I'm surprised, this is just not me. Maybe I'm just exhausted, I spent most of the night handling his pent up desires. It was hard work, handling his inexperience, one minute too gentle, the next too rough, and all the time too emotional. When it comes to the mechanics of sex, I prefer porn, I'm sure of it, it's just so much more efficient.

And amongst all that, I scanned his body whilst pretending to massage him. I felt not only his skin and bone – but also his body hair brushing the back of my hands – as if I'd slipped in between his body and his aura – ready to steal what information his body would offer up.

I let his body speak into my vision. Like a hawk, I hovered above an oak woodland spreading out in all directions. Through a gap in the tree cover I glimpsed a young man covered in dry scabs, sitting on a rock, holding a staff, unconcerned by the dark hairy pigs snuffling around in the undergrowth. There's a gust of wind, and as my feathered body rebalanced, a mist drifted in and it all faded.

The image left me feeling sad and I was still thinking about it when I fell asleep.

I unstick myself from Ben, he wakes up and turns to me.

'Hi.' His voice is quiet and dry.

I look into his face, 'Hi handsome.'

He leans in and lightly kisses me on the cheek. He pulls me closer, 'So what do we do now sexy?'

I roll away, 'You go and make me breakfast.'

He reaches out and cups a hand around my balls. 'Really?'

'Really.'

He swings himself out of bed, pulls on his boxers and wraps himself in a crumpled green dressing gown, 'I'll give you a shout when it's ready.'

I pull the duvet cover around me. He quietly closes the bedroom door behind him. I hear him go for a piss and then pad downstairs. I grab my phone and check the spy-cam recording. It's perfect. I send it across to Robinson. He'll diss my ethics, but he'll get off on it in so many ways.

Ben's made an effort – a bacon sarnie – I'm starving. June is shuffling around covered head to foot in one of those cloaks guys wear in Morocco. I've worked out that her bedroom is next to the kitchen, where the dining room used to be.

I pour her some coffee, 'June, do you remember

the city – like back in the 60s 70s?'

She picks up her mug, 'So different – some of the houses in the Circus, and the Crescent come to think of it, were run down, sometimes home to small communes of hippies. I preferred the place when it was like that. I moved away to be with his Mom and then came back to find this theme park.'

I sit there eating my sarnie, nodding.

Ben seems done with breakfast because he stands up and looks intent, 'I'm going to take a shower.'

I pour myself another coffee and carry on asking June about her life, anything to divert attention from her asking about mine.

When I head back upstairs, Ben's still in the shower. I go into the bedroom and crouch down next to my backpack. The zip on the main compartment is more open than before. I look inside. Yes, he's been snooping. I wonder what he made of the contents – a spare t-shirt, two pairs of socks, two pairs of briefs, a small plastic bag containing a toothbrush and razor, and my phone charger. Now he knows how light I'm travelling but I know more about him too, he's being cautious, he doesn't trust me, yet. I don't blame him. I better go and join him in the shower.

Chapter 17

After our shower I set up a stream of Patrick Keiller's London on the desktop then flop down next to him but avoid getting too close – I need him to concentrate.

Every time I watch 'London' I notice some new detail. In one shot, an army of suited and booted commuters are crossing Waterloo Bridge, walking towards the camera. Standing out from them, coming into focus – is a young guy with floppy blond hair. He's dressed casually and chews his nails as he walks towards the camera. He's hot and he's always caught my eye – but this time the narrator's voiceover grabs my attention – everyone acting so identically every day that their lives are effectively shorter than what's recorded.

I'm also drawn to the scene of the aftermath of the office bomb blast in The City, glaring yellowish strip lighting illuminating every floor – vertical blinds flapping in the blown out windows – flocks of paper riding the air currents.

I usually become bored and frustrated as the film drifts on, because just like Robinson, it becomes poetic and rambling. But today I'm picking up a darker vibe – of dreams snuffed out by hopelessness -

galvanising my resolve to do something.

The film ends and Ben lies there, brow furrowed, 'Did you hear when the narrator said that Robinson talked about the problem with London, the problem with the city?' There's a racing enthusiasm in his voice, 'That's why we're watching, yes?'

'Yes.'

Ben sighs, 'He's a real enigma, this Robinson. I like the way Keiller builds his character - almost as if he's an archetype.'

'Actually, Robinson told me he got depressed after this film came out, even more so after the two sequels. He thought that Keiller had skillfully depicted his ability to understand the city, the problem with the city, but.' I pause. 'But rather than express his vision as an optimistic rallying call, he claimed Keiller depicted hopelessness and futility. He was pissed with Keiller for that and they drifted apart after the films were released.'

'I know it was intentional not to, but I really wanted to see Robinson at some point in the film.'

'Robinson did too. He was angry that he was made unreal – invisible.'

'How did you meet Robinson?'

'Cruising in Finsbury Park – a year or so ago. Then we got talking.'

'How old is he? I imagine him as quite old.'

'Yeah he's a daddy for sure. A poor nomadic one.'

'What does he look like?'

I can't resist a smile, 'A bit like an older you.'

His sad eyes don't care for the comparison one bit, and I find myself backtracking, 'Well not really. He's slim but not in an athletic way like you. His face is gaunt like he's been smoking for way too many years, but his eyes are alert. And his clothes don't do him any justice, the same grimy hill-walking gear every day, the type of guy you see reading the papers in a local library on a wet Monday.'

Ben's body tenses, 'Did you, you know?'

'Oh yeah – he's got that something, especially when he talks - he's smooth, like irish cream - always teasing and tantalising with his cleverness and knowledge. I couldn't resist, not then.'

Ben hesitates, 'Are you still lovers?'

'Nah, we fell out over something. It's there in the film actually. I respect his analysis, even his visionary dreams. But that's his problem, he just dreams, he never takes any action. And he's tangled up in all that old poetry. And that part-time job at the uni holds him in check I reckon. And in the sequels later films, where he's walking out of the city I saw it as a kop out.'

Ben touches my hair with his fingers, 'It seems like he's had a huge impact on you.'

'His analysis has stuck with me – how through capitalism and the so-called good manners of English culture, the common man has been severed from the landscape, access, ownership, pushed into limbo spaces. But when he dreamt of artists and writers reclaiming the city, he never said what that would look like. I pleaded for action, to take back a city, to see what actually happened. He told me to come back when I'd identified a suitable place to take on and had a plan.'

'Is that why you're here?'

I wink at him.

'Are you still in touch even though you fell out? Is he still in London?'

'Don't know, don't care. I blocked him.'

I'm lying, Ben has to focus on me and what I do, not Robinson.

'So what now?' asks Ben.

'Later, we need to go into town just before it gets dark.'

'What for?'

'To watch the crowd.'

Chapter 18

The coffee is crap and I'm craving a ciggy but I'm sure we're in the right place and at the right time for what I'm looking for. Our table in front of the cafe overlooks the small busy square in the cheaper end of town near the bus station and the college. The sun is almost finished for the day, the light is tinged with blue – everything seems less defined, uncertain.

As I scan the people on the square, I nudge Ben with my knee, 'Stop looking at your phone.'

He puts it away and starts to follow my gaze, 'This must be the only cafe in the city open after six.'

'This 'city' is scared of the dark, scared of being a city. It's more like a village of inbreds where they can't wait to lock up and go to bed.'

But we're not quite there yet, the square is busy with what looks like locals. Two traders are dismantling their fruit and veg stall, the left-over produce already crated. A striped plastic tarpaulin lies folded on the floor next to them, only the rusty metal frame remains to be taken down.

'What are we looking for?' asks Ben.

'I'll know when I see it.'

There's a small group of street drinkers with their dogs, sitting on the floor outside the mini-supermarket on the corner. One of them shouts across the square to someone they know. A bench has been commandeered as a bike stand by a group of fast food delivery riders snatching a conversation between jobs. In front of a defence solicitor's office, a few ugly emo college kids, educational hangers on for sure, stand around vaping whilst looking at their feet.

Around this collection of living statues, others are on the move, criss crossing the cobbled square. Office workers, mostly women, are heading towards the cheaper housing estates on the other side of the river. A steady stream of smartly dressed older couples come from the direction of the multi-story car-park, briskly passing us, no doubt on their way to pre-theatre restaurant suppers. Lycra'd women and shorted men are heading to the nearby gym.. A young man and woman, both in restaurant-bar black basics, come out of the dodgy block of flats near the city's only chip shop. They pause in the square, kiss briefly before parting and heading off up separate streets.

Ben has got his eyes on the street drinkers, 'It's a bit edgy around here isn't it?'

I laugh, 'For this city, maybe. What's good though, this is definitely a crossing point between 'your' city and the other side, which no one ever talks about, you know, that area beyond the student houses, near the football ground.'

'Yes, the Georgian buildings pretty much end here, though they used to extend a bit further.'

'If we're gonna find what we're looking for, we're

gonna find it here.'

'What exactly?'

'That's a little test for you, to work it out. Oh, hold on, here we go.'

I've spotted someone crossing the square – taking loping strides in heavily scuffed skateboard trainers, vaping to hell on a long black pen-like device, their slim body swamped by some kind of hoodie-khagaul thing. Their face is shaded by a dark floppy hat-cap. Slung around their neck and hanging down across their hip is an old newspaper delivery bag advertising The Sunday People. They pass the radio station before disappearing down some steps.

I hesitate to get up and follow them, even though the twinge in my gut is telling me to.

'What were you staring at?' asks Ben.

'Damn, they've gone now. Did you see them, with that strange hat on? Fuck - I should have gone with my instinct.'

Ben points to the pelican crossing, 'Do you mean him, the one with a weird walk?'

I sit up in my chair, 'Yes!'

He comes in our direction, covering the ground quickly, dodging around people, still vaping hard. Unruly blonde hair pokes out from under that ridiculous hat. His face looks pale, almost raw, especially around his thin red lips. But when I see the black eyes, that fixed stare aimed at nothing or no-one in particular, as if he's staring into a void - I know I've found what I was looking for.

As he passes I grab Ben and whisper, 'Don't take your eyes off him.'

Ben's eyes show that the penny has dropped for him too, 'Ahhh, The Man of the Crowd?'

'Yes.'

Our 'Man' goes into a hardware shop.

'Is there another entrance to that place?' I ask.

'No idea.'

I watch the entrance, trying to remember what Robinson had told me about this archetype – that such people were like guides into another world, that they were worth following - talking with them if you can. Robinson claimed he'd identified and talked to a few in the past, usually in shopping centres. And this one's cute in a weirdo way, that's a bonus. But he definitely doesn't look approachable and there's an uncertainty about him.

After a few minutes he comes back out - the newspaper bag looks fuller. What's he bought? He stops for a moment, I get my phone out, ready to take a photo on the sly but they glance in my direction and I hold back.

The street lights start to flicker on – Our 'Man' turns their back on the square and heads off up the theatre street. I push back my chair, 'Come on, stalker time.'

He's not hard to follow – as he passes through

the lion gates into the park, he takes a side path with hedge cover but Ben's local knowledge enables us to walk parallel.

'Why are we doing this?' asks Ben.

'I just wanna see what they're doing, OK?'

'I don't like it.' Ben's voice has a bitter edge.

We seem to be heading towards The Crescent and he does indeed turn onto the wide pavement that runs along the front of the city's set-piece. It's properly dusk now and there's hardly anyone else on the path, most of the tourists have left.

Ben guides me by the elbow, 'Let's pretend to walk across the parkland in front.'

We go through a small gateway into a wide open green that sits between the park and The Crescent. There's still quite a few people here, beefy boys and debs, finishing off picnics, down to the last beer or prosecco. Like cattle grazing on pasture. One group of jocks are throwing a rugby ball to each other. We pass through the scene unnoticed.

Above us, 'Man of the Crowd' has stopped in front of one of the grand houses on The Crescent, the windows all boarded up from the inside with wooden shutters.

'Closed up or not, I never see anyone going in or out of these places.' says Ben.

'I was going to ask if you knew anyone who lives here, or if you ever kopped off with anyone from here.'

Ben coughs a derisory laugh.

Our 'Man' starts walking again and we follow as he

slips around the corner of the crescent. He's walking faster now, occasionally looking up at the buildings that abut onto the crescent. He doesn't seem to have noticed us. He follows the row of old 'artisan' buildings around – essentially forming a high wall broken up occasionally with painted garage doors. What windows there are, are well above head height.

When a smaller, poorer green appears, we walk onto it pretending to divert away from him. There's a couple giving their two dogs a run. One dog, a terrier of some sort, sniffs around a clump of silver birches.

Our Man keeps following the wall as it bends again towards the other end of the crescent. I hold us back, that street he's in is too quiet, it would be way too obvious.

I whisper to Ben, 'This wall in front of us, is it still part of the crescent complex?

'Yes, we're on the servant side.'

'It's like a fucking fortress – dressed up as a Georgian cake.'

'It's always reminded me of Castel St Angelo, Hadrian's mausoleum.'

I've no idea what he's on about and there's no time to ask, 'Shit, he's coming back this way.'

We drop onto a park bench and sit there pretending to look at our phones.

When he reaches the curve of the back wall nearest us, our Man stops and takes something out of his bag. I can't see what it is but then they shake it and I hear a familiar dull metallic clicking.

His arm arcs in front of the wall along with the hiss of the aerosol. He reaches back into his bag and switches cans, and adds to his design – it's all over in seconds and he lopes off.

We hurry to where he was - it's some tag in black and orange that makes no sense – circles bisected by arrows, a string of digits. I take a few shots with my phone but there's no time to think as we set off again to catch up with him.

We follow him back across town, towards the train station. Just past the mail depot, he takes a turn into a street of terraced red brick houses, and disappears from view. We halt at the corner.

'Maybe he lives here.' whispers Ben.

'I didn't hear a door go, did you?'

The street is empty and poorly lit. The front doors are worn out, most of the doorbells look like botch jobs. Weeds grow on some of the doorsteps. Just two cars parked on the street.

'Don't turn around.' whispers Ben, 'I think he's standing in the window just down the road, looking at us.'

'Ok. Let's go but tell you what, I wanna know the story of this place.'

As we walk back home I'm excited that I can report my sighting of the Man in the Crowd to Robinson. I feel like we've made a big step forward. He knows we have found him. Will he join us?

Chapter 19

I'm on our bed looking into space. Ben is at the desk, poring over a web page. 'You were more or less right, Manny, about Taunton Street, they were council houses, the first built in the city. 'Listen to this, they chose red brick and not the local ashlar to mark them out as social housing.'

'But what about the other streets around there? They're built of honey stone but they look just as poor.'

'It says here, when they expanded the estate they realised those newer houses would be seen from the train crossing the viaduct above, so they switched materials, to maintain the heritage image of the city.'

'This is some nasty fucked up place! Ben, how are we going to rebel against this city?'

'Rebellion? Aren't you taking this a bit far?'

'You were up for it when we chatted online,' I glare at him.

He comes over and sits on the edge of the bed, 'I still feel like an outsider but maybe I wasn't so happy then. Now we've found each other.'

I found you more like, I think. 'Love is the drug, eh?'

'If you like.'

'This place - I wanna fuck it over.'

'But it's a city.' He moves closer, and rests his head on my shoulder, 'Really, how are we going to do that?'

'I'll think of something, I'm sure. And however small the impact - things will be different after.'

'Is it the right way to go about your project - to rebel?'

'In my world, yes. There was always meant to be an activist element to it all as far as I can work out. Anyway, never mind the city right now, let me start with you first.'

He smiles, 'Oh yeah?'

I start to undo his shirt, 'But you've got to do what I say.'

He slides his hand up my thigh, 'Yes boss.'

I undo another button on his shirt, 'And I don't just mean now, but till we see this project through.'

Ben pauses, 'Well.'

I tug at his open shirt, 'Get these clothes off. I want to give you a massage.'

'Mmm.' He moans as he starts undressing.

'Now, face down.'

He does as he's told. I get up off the bed and strip down to my pants. I'm going to rescan him, see if I can get any more details. And for the hell of it, I use my phone to switch the cam on.

I take my time with the scan. It's the same scene as

before but the teenager is kneeling, his hands resting on a large lump of stone, that's all I get.

Afterwards, I lie next to him thinking about the stone - I've encountered it before. I turn the image over and over in my mind until I remember.

I slip out of bed and get on the computer. I rewind through the Keiller film until I find the scene in The City of London - a metal grille set into a wall, protecting – there it is! The lump of worked stone is hardly visible but I'm sure it's what I've just seen scanning Ben, though I can't make out what the narrator is saying, no matter how many times I replay the clip. Then I find a transcript online and reading it knocks the breath out of me. Why didn't Robinson tell me about this?!

Chapter 20

The suburban roads have petered out into lanes and the pavements have disappeared. I step up onto a stile built and take in the English countryside – the pretty hamlet set in a patchwork of deep green fields. This isn't nature, this is industrial farmland. But then there's the big hill across the valley.

'So what's the plan?' asks Ben.

I look over my shoulder, 'Remember what I said last night?'

'Do what you say. Just go with it.' he whines.

He follows me as I cross the stile, ignore the waymarked path and take the fainter, more direct track towards a clump of hawthorn down next to the brook at the bottom of the field. The ground is summer dry and the short tough grass drags on my feet.

The further we drop into the valley the more impressive the big hill looks. I feel calm out here. It's not exactly the type of hinterland I go for, but the city is out of sight and I can feel my thoughts and strength building.

The dense ring of hawthorns on both sides of the brook seem to mark a crossing or at least a watering spot - entered down a track next to a holly bush. I feel a vibration of excitement as I lead us in.

The space opens up, hawthorn branches forming a shady canopy above us. The surface of the fast running brook is dark and sparkly.

I stop, 'It's special here. Important for the project. I just know.'

'It looks a bit muddy. You should've borrowed my old walking boots.'

I shake my head. Having these trainers on makes me feel like Robinson is here, feeling the landscape with me, witnessing my work.

I walk down to the 'beach', remove the trainers then socks and throw them across the brook. They land beyond the mud on the other side.

Ben points upstream, 'There's a footbridge just up there.'

'Yeah, but then we wouldn't get to do this.'

I roll up the jeans I've borrowed from Ben as far as I can and slowly wade into the black water. The brook is colder and more powerful than I expect, already tugging at my ankles, the dull pain of random large pebbles pressing into the soles of my feet. It soon gets too deep and I wade back.

Ben laughs, 'Given up?'

I pull my t-shirt over my head and off and unbuckle the belt on my jeans. In seconds, I'm bollock naked, my clothes in a small pile on the ground. 'Pass me the bag.'

I reach for his jeans belt and he steps back, 'Really?'

'Really.'

I watch him as he undresses, his actions are awkward. He looks around.

'Nobody's coming' I reassure him 'And so what if they do. We're just naturists in a quiet spot.'

I stuff our clothes into the backpack and throw it across to the other side. I take him by the hand and lead him into the water.

Ben squeals at the cold, then starts to relax, I watch him look up at the hawthorn, taking in the shards of light and the patterns of the water. He turns to me with a grin, 'This is amazing! I feel so alive.'

At the halfway point the water is up to our waists and we're having to clutch eachothers arms in an effort to remain upright.

'You OK sexy boy?' I ask.

'It's a bit late to ask that.'

We wade toward the other side.

When the water shallows to ankle deep I stop, 'Wait.'

I look down at the clayish mud and imagine it pumping up from deep inside the earth. I stoop and dredge up a handful of it.. I then break some off and begin to smear it onto his chest.

'Are you crazy!?' Ben exclaims.

'Ben, Ben, Ben.' I say gently as I smear on more, matting the mud with his body hair like wattle and daub, 'Cummon, do me.'

Ignoring that he's getting hard, I smear the clay onto his cock. We finish with each other's faces, step out of the water, and do our own feet.

We look at each other. This means something.

I pick up our shoes and bag as we emerge from under the hawthorn canopy and into the bright afternoon sunshine.

'Let's lie here, we'll be in full sun.'

'Caked in mud?'

'Seriously, no more questions.'

Chapter 21

The sun and the warm breeze has dried the mud on my back to a crispy shell. I flip over and within minutes I feel the mud constricting across my chest and around my nipples. Ben is asleep next to me.

That smearing, I think of it as a preparation, for something raw that will happen. It's not a mask, I've worn enough of those to know.

I get to my feet and shards of dried earth splinter from me as my body flexes. I look down at Ben, he looks wiry now that his body hair is matted closely to his body – his smooth cock stands out, its porcelain sheath still moist.

I step forward and cast a shadow over him, 'Time to move on.'

He slowly opens his eyes, dazed, and looks around.

I pick up the backpack, 'Let's get dressed, leave the mud on.'

We dress slowly, I look up towards the Hill.

The path takes us through the picturesque hamlet. An old lady stands at her front gate tending a clump of hollyhocks. OK, so our faces are caked in mud, but well before greeting distance, probably before she's noticed the mud, she turns away until we pass.

After we pass the last cottage, we reach a place where several tracks meet. Ben consults his OS map, 'That book you got mentioned a major intersection of the old pre-Roman lanes and paths, looks like we've found it. Now, which one to take?'

'Ben, the hill is up there in front of us, let's follow the landscape, how about that track over there?'

We curl gently upwards, following a path along the edge of a broad meadow with open views back across the valley. Five minutes later we reach a junction surrounded by small gnarled trees barely in leaf, clearly disfigured by years of exposure to winter winds.

'It's muddy here. Is that from livestock?' I ask.

'It might be one of the natural springs – the book said there are four around the hill.'

I point to a clear gap in the scrubby treeline just above us, 'Up there do you reckon?'

'Yes, I'm pretty sure this is one of the old entrances to the settlement.'

It doesn't look much like a path, but we're able to zig zag up and over an earthwork rampart and across a man-made ditch onto the summit.

We're standing on the edge of a large flat disc of meadow about 300m in diameter. The air is noisy and it brushes against my eyeballs. I see a worn path around the perimeter of the plateau. Two people are walking dogs on the other side. I turn towards the centre of the summit and begin to take careful steps into the untouched longer grass. 'Tread where I tread and watch out for bird nests.'

'When we reach the middle, I'm surprised to find a slight hollow. I drop to my knees - the perimeter isn't visible now. I lie down on my back and beckon Ben to join me. I feel the shape of the hollow holding my body, as if I'm being spooned by a giant daddy. I know, in this moment, that the hill holds the answers to our project.

'What are we doing, Manny?'

'Shhhh. Listen.'

The air in the hollow is still though I can still hear the air rushing above us. Then, his song cuts through the air as he moves through the sky. Ben nudges me. I listen harder trying to locate him. On the third reprise Ben points to a black spot in song, ascending into the sky, then dropping like Icarus to the ground, then rising again.

'Skylark.' Ben whispers 'It's beautiful.'

He's right, but I'm not playing into his romantic fantasy. That bird's ancestors must have been the inspiration and the warning to Bladud.

My focus turns to what is under me. I'm so into this place, I'm feeling ravenous to tear into the grass with my teeth, gobble up the dirt, stuff my face with this hill, all the way down to the stream we just bathed in.

Ben turns and looks into my eyes, with that mud smeared face, 'Manny.'

It's time now, for us both to emerge renewed and revitalised from this wet earth.

I let him initiate a kiss but only as a lead into what I need - I undo his jeans and release his hard cock, the smeared mud on it still moist. I lean over and slide my mouth down over the full length of him – my way to eat this landscape, swallow it, digest it, make it a part of me. As I suck him I dig a small hole in the earth with my hands, between his legs by my knees. I unzip myself and work him with one hand, me with the other. And as our timing comes together, he shoots into my mouth and I guide my offering into the hill.

Chapter 22

We sit cross legged, facing each other.

'Why are we here? It's not just romance is it?' asks Ben.

'Sucking your muddy cock?' I laugh. 'No, there was something in the film. I missed it so many times because of the way the narrator pronounced it. You remember that lump of stone behind a metal grille in a wall in The City?'

'Vaguely.'

'When he says that Robinson held it to be of such great importance that the bus route to it had a reverential, almost religious significance for him.'

'Oh yeah. Outlandish.'

'That's the Bladud Stone, Bladud from around here. I went back and checked, several times over.'

'So?'

'In myth, Bladud had magical powers, including flying.' I try to stay calm, 'It's believed his original city was here, where we are now. He flew from here before crashing to his death at the spot marked by the stone - the site of a Roman temple, as it happens.

Ben leans back and looks at me, surprised, 'I didn't know you were into this mythology stuff?'

'I'm not. I'd get pissed off when Robinson started

talking like this, tying himself in knots, getting away from the point, but.' and I point towards the city, 'Well, before that pile of shit over there, something was here.'

'You're tapping into an older psychogeography?'

'Not just that. I think of here as a kind of gateway into the city, a way to get under its skin, something like that.'

'Did Robinson ever say anything about here?'

'No, only that the city was a good choice. I thought he was talking about its small size, but maybe he was referring to this Bladud connection.'

'So, you think exploring the city's deeper history is going to help?'

I nod, looking at my trainers, wondering what Robinson would think of this change in my thinking. He'd probably be amused, though I'm starting to think he wanted me to discover this.

I stumble on with my idea, 'Bladud was definitely an outsider, queer I reckon, though I've got no evidence for that. I dunno, I feel he's helping me to understand the city at its core.'

Ben rubs some dried mud off his arm, 'All this mud bathing and bird watching is about Bladud? I thought it might be about us, you know, getting closer.'

I put my hands on his shoulders 'You're my partner on this project, aren't you? How much closer can you get?' I lean forward and kiss him gently on the lips.

Ben rubs his eyes and laughs, 'Crazy guy.'

After we retrace our steps back to the perimeter path, we follow the earthworks around to the trig point, where we get a good view toward the city.

Ben points, 'Look. The brook is down there, and my house is just over the brow of that rise.'

I'm idly gazing at the inscribed brass plate fitted into the surface of the trig point – showing the directions of various landmarks.

Ben looks over my shoulder, 'Of course! That tag, that 'Man of the Crowd' spray painted behind the Crescent, I bet it's a digital coordinate.'

He checks the photos then some app before showing me, 'Yes, it's the coordinates for that spot.'

'Clever.'

'Perhaps we should find him again, he might be interested in what we're doing.'

'I know, I've got it in hand.'

Ben sits down on the lip of the rampart – I sit down next to him, we lean into each other and get close. I like it.

Ben opens his backpack and takes out the book which he's wrapped in a tea-towel, 'The Records Office would have a fit if they knew we had brought this here.'

'They'll be lucky to get it back.'

Ben scans the pages, 'It says precious little about the settlement but oh, here you go, 'The jury is out on its actual function during the Iron Age though its defensive earthworks remain clearly visible and the presence of wells within the fortification would suggest habitation was possible.'

I gesture towards the city, 'The Clerk showed me a geophysical survey which suggested a fortified village of metal workshops - small buildings not just here on the plateau but all the way down the hillside beyond this defensive ditch. I wonder what happened?'

'The book doesn't say much except that it was common land at the time of writing and had been for hundreds of years. Now it's owned by the National Trust.'

I take out my phone and stare blankly at the city through the camera app and zoom in – the diocese flag flutters atop the elongated flagpole, probably still the highest point in the city. I turn to Ben, 'Do you think the landscape, even a landscape like this, can reflect aspects of queerness? It's something I've been thinking about. I mean 10% of us are gay-queer right? Are there any signs of us? I mean all of this, this surface countryside has been shaped by man, no?'

'You mean like cruising areas in parks, the tracks?'

'Yes, but out here.'

'Well there's Beckford Tower over there, and his pink sarcophagus next to it, but he was rich. No, It can't just be about the marks on the landscape can it? Especially being a minority, which we are – it's about how we see it, how we move through it, how we use it.

'I suppose you're right but it just doesn't seem enough.' I sigh, "Anyway, what does the book say about Bladud?'

'Give me a minute.'

Ben flicks through the pages until he finds what he was looking for, 'Here, that he built a Temple to Apollo – that's about it.'

I blow air out through my lips, 'I'm not going to find the answer scrabbling around in history books. That's just what Robinson would do! There must be another way.'

We both sit gazing towards the city.

'Ben, I know your Mum lives here but why do you live here? Are you her carer?'

His left foot twitches as if he's about to kick out, 'Kind of – but she didn't ask or expect me to – it just happened.'

'But what about you? This city is not your tribe is it?'

'You know it isn't.'

'Not anyone here at all?'

Ben shakes his head, his eyes look sad, 'If I do make any friends, they tend to be incomers, academics and the like, attracted by the beauty of the place, but if they're single, they sense the danger of boredom and the stuff we've talked about and leave after a year or two.'

'Why don't you leave?'

He looks horrified, 'Mum. I...she's getting on a bit now.'

'You have to wait for her to die then? Or give her up to a care home at some point.'

I see his eyes burning, 'Sorry, Ben, that came out

all wrong. I don't even know why I brought it up.'

'It's OK.' he says, but he looks deflated.

I stand up and offer my hand to pull him up, 'Is there another way down, from the hill?'

Ben nods towards the slope dropping off to our left, 'See that National Trust sign, we can take those steps down to the car park and join the lane.'

As we descend the earthen steps, two 4x4s pull into the tiny car park. Identical families pour out of the vehicles – two small children each plus a baby strapped in across the mothers' chests, plus four King Charles spaniels or something. They pile up the path, talking loudly, their dogs unleashed as if they were on their own private estate. The children look like the spaniels – squidgy faces and floppy blond hair. The group is oblivious to us until the parents see our muddied faces - then the children are shepherded past us with disapproving glances. For sure, these people and those like them represent this city and they need to be taught a lesson.

'Didn't the book say there were battles fought here?' I ask.

'Yes, there's even mention of Alfred the Great. Kingdoms changed hands.'

'I like the sound of that. This hill, Ben, we're gonna make it ours, soon enough.'

Chapter 23

From the moment we left The Hill I could feel energy draining away from me. It felt like an exhausting trudge back. I'd hauled myself into the shower like some zombie and by the time I'd scrubbed and washed the mud away my head was blank. Now, as I stand in front of the bookcase, the blankness has become something darker and more brooding. And the Ben thing is out of control. Even though I engineered his infatuation with me, I don't know what to do next and whether I even needed it.

Ben comes in, wrapped in a towel, his hair still wet. He stands behind me and wraps his arms around my waist., 'Today, up there on the Hill, was really special.'

'Yeah.' My tone way too flat to hide my feelings.

I feel him tense.

I try for some positivity, 'Look, I need to think. Can I use the spare room?'

Stillness, 'Sure.'

'Like, for a day or two.'

'Sleep in there as well?'

I nod.

'But why? I thought things were ... and we're really getting somewhere with the project.' his voice is cracking.

'Like I said, I just need to think, OK?'

He takes his arms away from me and steps back, 'So you turn up unannounced, talk me into letting you stay and now you want your own room!'

I've been here before, people thinking I'm just something for the weekend. I've learned the best way is to stay quiet.

Chapter 24

The spare room is at the front of the house. My eye runs down the street that, like some ley line, points directly to the Abbey, the so-called heart. I'm overwhelmed by this city right now, almost powerless to stop being dragged down into it. I pull the curtains shut and try to get back to my research.

I'm not done with Bladud, I'm skipping through web pages, cherry picking stories. According to Geoffrey of Monmouth, Bladud was the first king of the Britons to practise magic – using alchemy to create the hot spring baths through alchemy – sacrificing a man to the devil every year in payment for tending the fire.

And on his fateful flight, Bladud fell from the sky onto the Temple of Apollo in Trinovantum, the original name for London – where he was dashed to bits. I imagine him, inspired by ancestors of the skylarks we saw yesterday, but in his hubris Bladud forgot to consider how he would handle their Icarus-like descent.

And me? Nomadic - homeless, with not much more than Robinson's red trainers to my name. I'm meant to be finding 'the authentic artistic me' and I'm still faking it – kidding myself I can reinvent psychogeography – use it as the tool for the political change it was intended for, and in the process prove myself to Robinson. Seriously, What planet am I on? All I've done is invaded this home, got lonely, desperate Ben to fall for me, as I fall down a rabbit hole of mythology that's as ridiculous as any religion.

And now it's all unravelling.

And I risk I'm getting sucked into Ben's world. I was happier before, running away.

And that city out there - I can't do anything about that.

I consider messaging Robinson but I feel my head and then my body shutting down, I drag myself across to the single bed and give myself up.

Chapter 25

Two days have passed, my waking hours the same as my sleep, blank. I've only left this room to piss and shit, picking up the food and drink Ben's been leaving outside my door on my way back. I've not looked at my phone, laptop, or read anything.

I went to Ben's room last night – to make amends with a shag - a disaster. Within minutes I was just laying there letting him do his stuff.

He picked up on my indifference, 'Hey, how about giving me one of your special massages, they take me to somewhere else, they really do.'

I shook my head – he looked wounded.

'Manny, it seems like you're in a dark place right now, just come back to bed, it might help.'

I looked blankly at him.

His insecurity seemed to ripple in his brown eyes, then swim into his mouth, 'Is it something I've done?'

I look down at my toes, past my limp cock. I couldn't take it anymore. I needed the blankness. I got up to leave and at the door turned around. 'Would it be better if I told you I preferred porn and that us having sex is just for the project?'

Chapter 26

It passed – the weakness has gone. I open the curtains, the sun is high – late morning?

I message Ben, 'Sorry. I needed to put myself back together.' I add a gif of humpty dumpty.

He replies with a confused head emoji.

I reply with a hug.

He sends a heart.

I look down at the city, 'You've done this to me. I'm not going to leave without doing something to you.'

I have breakfast with June. She's quiet but friendly. Back in the spare room, I go through my photos, video diary and notes. I scan through last night's webcam footage - at one point he's at his desk, watching porn, jerking off. I think about joining him, I even start idly sucking on my big toe but I change my mind and fast forward till he cums. But I feel calmer, I'm able to think.

What would Robinson think of my progress? He probably would have read this place deeper and more intellectually than me but he can't taste the dirt of the city like I can. He would have wheeled out his usual pipe-dream of artistic communities arising, but in no way helping to make that happen. I imagine him concluding that this city is too small to generate such communities. Maybe that's why he didn't discourage me from coming here – maybe he wants me to fail.

I start pacing around the room. I know I might get it very wrong, but unlike him, I'm going to do something. All I know is that it's going to be about The Hill, a kind of disorientation. But first, I need to get out and walk the city, alone.

Chapter 27

I walk to the other side, south of the river. Cheap bedsits sit above even cheaper breakfast joints, white vans pulled up onto the pavements outside. A dank passage under the railway viaduct has led me up to the football stadium, its corrugated iron shell placarded with adverts for local businesses. I was hoping for a bit of 'life' but it's a ghost town. The car park next to the stadium is empty except for a couple of old guys stepping around a people carrier, one crouching every now and then to inspect the bodywork. I'm so bored, I wander back towards the train station.

Cowper Street doesn't even look like a street, more an extended forecourt to a garage offering cheap MOTs but something draws me in. Somehow hidden from sight of the main road is a row of blackened and unkempt two-storey lock-ups squeezed under all but one of the arches of the railway viaduct. I like this place and I start taking photos.

I hear a raucous laugh, then, emerging through the clear archway, a woman in her 40's say, with short bleached blond hair and a tall guy in a pale green tracksuit with short dark dreads and a big smile. He looks much much younger than her. It's her laugh I heard, he's kinda giggling.

I have the measure of him already and I can see from just the slightest movement of his eyes that he's taken me in as well. She's unsteady on her feet as they approach the door of the first lock-up, and she seems to pause to reassess the situation. The lad smiles then elbows the door open. I watch intently as they exchange a few words and enter. From here it looks like a right doss-house, worse than that – derelict – she must like it dirty.

After about a minute, curiosity gets the better of me and I wander over towards the open door of the den. I peer in – empty beer bottles, discarded needles, screwed up tissues, litter blown in from the street. It smells of piss. I can hear the low groans of their lovemaking coming from upstairs. I cross the threshold and look in at the first open doorway - an office desk, a broken chair and a dirty mattress on the stone floor. The place must be riven with vermin. I stand there, staring at a piece of old peeling wallpaper, a country cottage design, listening to them, her groans an indication of his thrusts. I think about him - how I might get into his head. As they finish I step back outside and walk along the row of lock-ups, taking pictures.

I see them come out. They stop, he caresses her face, she opens her bag and passes him some banknotes and hurries back through the archway. Seconds later I hear a door, a car pulling away. He leans against the wall and takes out a pack of cigarettes. He notices me and tilts the packet in my direction. I start to walk towards him. I need to make some connections in this city.

Chapter 28

He's called Tom, he works part-time at one of the greasy spoon cafes, topping up a below minimum wage with sex work. We get on and he helps me bulk up my network with hippy-chick art students, also the 'car' dealers from outside the stadium who can supply everything a party needs, plus a collection of likely lads from Grindr. He ropes in the trafficked 'staff' from the nail bars in town. It's working - the numbers are looking good. He's even put me in contact with 'Man of the Crowd who won't give his name and only communicates in gifs. When I asked Tom about it he laughed, said he's the same with everyone, and never speaks either.

In my wanderings I pick up more collaborators - the barman-come-bouncer that works in the dodgy corner shop by day, chinese casino by night – the guy that hawks his grandmothers samosas from a barrow up and down Market street – the woman that runs the Cuban cafe with her spanish husband and wonders how they fuck they ended up here – the weight lifting hotel night manager who wishes he never left Krakow - the widow with her part-time job as dog walker, pulled here and there by pedigrees, each one worth more than her battered Volvo estate that she ferries them around in.

And Man of the Crowd reaches people beyond even Tom's or my reach. Outsiders lurking in the frozen food supermarket or the bingo hall. People who live on dilapidated canal boats or in nearby woods, some hidden even deeper in the landscape. None of these people know they are connected yet. But they will, very soon.

Chapter 29

       As I'm walking back to Ben's, daydreaming, I step out onto the zebra crossing without looking. A lipstick red sports car comes to a sudden halt in front of me. I look up in alarm, about to raise a hand in apology. And there they are, together. The Duchess grips the wheel, scowling at me. Her passenger, Arran, still recognisable in shades, sneers.

I lower my head trying to hide my surprise and continue my crossing. The black and white strips undulate and I put out my arms to hold my balance. The car growls and lurches closer, the orange beacon flashing in my eyes. I stumble to the halfway point and they shoot past me.

I look towards the receding car, my pulse is racing.

I figure they must be related. They both get to me, her more than him. She's onto me in some way. I just know it. It's as if that cold bony finger has broken through my skull and read my game-plan directly.

Chapter 30

I come off a call with Robinson and hurl my phone at the bed – it bounces off the mattress and onto the floor. What a messed up twat! He does my head in when he's on one.

I hear a gentle knock at the door – so polite. 'Yeah.' I snap. I'm feeling nasty, like paper when it cuts. Ben's looking all loving – time to wipe that right off his face.

He comes over and rests his hands on my waist, 'Someone upset you?'

I pull him to me, hard already and I feel that part of him responding. He brings his mouth towards my neck. I feel a tingle as he breezes hot breath just below my ear, just like Robinson would do. My temple throbs and that blush of mine shoots. I grip his shoulders and press down, he resists. I rough him. Now he's on his knees, looking up at me. I unzip and take it to him – pushing him back against the wall. I stare down at the city as I fuck his face. I slap him - like Robinson would me.

Why do I always want to impress that saggy old loser? When Robinson and me argued, sex always worked, I always had that over him, my desirability. But this time he went too far. What did he say? – 'You're not well read enough, you lack nuance, you're using fake psychogeography as a trojan horse for your own issues.'

I push myself deeper into Ben's throat until he starts to gag and tries to push me back. I give him a brief moment to breathe then grip his head hard.

I'd hit back though, 'Say's you – playing the enigma – you're impotent. Just like all the other middle aged guys who walk around London, divining the problems of society, then doing nothing about it.'

That had shut him up.

I look down at Ben, his eyes are pleading, watering.

I know why Robinson had had a go. He didn't like it one bit that I'd worked out the Bladud stone. Tough, he should have followed it up himself if it had meant so much to him. This is my domain - I'll do what I want.

Chapter 31

June is pottering around the garden in a lurid green tent of a summer dress, printed with wide orange chevrons which seem to push out from her mass like pulses of raw energy.

I'm sitting under King Apple, furiously group messaging on my phone.

'You're busy.' she comments.

'I'm organising something for the Solstice – a surprise for Ben, I'm doing it now, whilst he's out. Actually, I could do with your help.'

'Me?' she chuckles.

I pick up one of the Local Life magazines I've brought out from the conservatory and turn to the society pages. I lean across towards her and scan my finger across a page of photos taken at some business awards event. 'Can you tell me about these people, do you know any of them?'

She reads the names printed underneath each photograph, 'George and Anabella Dawson. Oh he's local old money married into the Portuguese aristocracy.'

Her finger slides to the next image, 'Cruikshank. Don't know them. Why are you asking anyway?'

I stay all casual, 'I'm involved in organising a picnic.'

She studies me intently, 'And you want to invite people like this? Hardly your scene.'

'I'm reaching out - bringing people together.'

She puts the open magazine down on the table, folds her arms across her chest and huffs. I know she wants me to tell her why but this is a test of trust.

'I want a select group invited, via that Yes Sir! delivery service, you know it? But I'm nobody here.'

'And I am?' she laughs.

'Well you were brought up here and you've been back a few years. I thought you might know people.'

'I suppose I do, if you put it like that. I know folks from the Friends Meeting House, they're pretty well connected – also maybe from Carnival fundraisers I was involved in five years ago.'

'Maybe now is the time to dust off the cobwebs for a good cause.'

She looks up into King Apple, as if the answer is up there in his branches.

She looks back at me, 'Who? Where? When?'

I smile and pick up my phone, 'Let's make a list.'

'The afternoon of the Solstice? That's in just over a week. No pressure.' June says. She picks up her phone, scrolls and taps then lifts it to her ear, 'Hello Nancy. June, June Taylor here... I know. I know. I'm not dead yet. Haah haah haah.'

June waves me away, I get up and walk towards the

117

kitchen.

She continues, 'Yes, very select, 25 parties max, a fundraiser yes...can you get the invites out in the next day or so, hand delivered... Yes Sir! They're perfect for something like this don't you think?'

I watch through the kitchen window as June leans over the magazine, pointing I guess at individual photos and relaying the names to Nancy, whoever she is. After a few minutes June puts her mobile on the table and beckons me over.

When I get to her she's beaming with pride, 'Sorted. Local Life will sponsor it and pay for the invites!'

I feel a thrill go deep into my stomach, dark and spicy. I instinctively give her a hug, realising that this is the first time I've ever touched her.

She laughs and gently pushes me away, 'Get away with you.'

I look back at her, 'Remember, I want it to be a surprise for Ben.'

She nods, but with a sad serious smile, 'Why are you doing it, Manny?'

'This Solstice thing? Cause I have to.'

'No, I meant Ben.'

'Same reason.'

She looks confused for a moment, shrugs, then slowly pushes herself up from her chair and lumbers off into the house. I message Tom and confirm the details – now it's time to connect our network.

Chapter 32

I open my eyes, I must've fallen asleep, 'cause I'm still in the deck chair under King Apple. Ben is standing in his bedroom window looking sad and a bit lost. I take a slow breath and get up. When I reach his door I knock gently.

'Yeah.' he says quietly.

I go in and stand next to him. His hands are resting on the windowsill, I touch the back of his hand. 'Hi.'

'What have you been doing?' he asks.

'Nothing much, chillin 'in the garden.'

'You look more relaxed anyway.'

'What dreams and hopes did you have when you were younger?'

"That's a change of subject.'

'Cummon.'

'Well, I wanted to live in Manchester. Purely based on photos I'd seen in New Musical Express, the bands, the clubbing. And then I applied to Uni there, and got in.'

'Had you ever been there?'

'Not before the interview. Mom and Mum took me up in the car and I just followed them around.'

'Did it live up to expectations?'

'Yes, I suppose. I gravitated towards the darker, monochrome parts of the city. Pubs with old punks and all that.'

'June likes it here doesn't she?'

Ben nods, 'She says she doesn't like the people much but I think she understands them at a deeper level.'

'Better the devil you know.'

I put my arm around his waist, 'But you. You're lost here.'

'Yeah. But I don't mind being lost, you know. But I don't like being ignored. Even when I was new in Manchester, I still felt heard. You know what I mean? There seemed to be space and spaces to live my life. That's what made the place so special for me. It wasn't just about being in a big city.

I think maybe I need to find my Manchester but I keep it to myself.

Ben continues, 'You know something? Even this dump had something once. In the 70s it formed one of the first Lesbian and Gay Foundation chapters in the country.'

'Well that revolutionary flame fizzled out.'

'Is there any hope to relight that flame?'

'We'll see.'

Ben turns into me and rests his hands on my shoulders, 'Can I ask you a question?'

'Sure.'

'Where's home, you know, when you're not doing this stuff?'

'It's not important.'

'Do you live with Robinson?'

'What's this all about? Feeling jealous or something?'

'Well do you?'

I take his hands off my shoulders, 'No. I stayed with him, I never lived with him.'

'How long?'

'What does it matter to you?'

'Manny, sorry, I'm getting this all wrong. Wait. I need to put it another way.' His voice goes lower, 'Are you homeless?'

I step back, my face burns as if I've been branded, 'Do you wanna give me a technical definition of that word, homeless?'

'Manny, if you're worried about where you'll stay after this project ends, you can stay longer here. I could talk with Mum.'

'Oh thank you for your charity offering this poor nomad a home? Do you think that when I'm finished with you I'll want to stick around?'

He looks wounded, 'Oh Manny, sorry, sorry. Forget what I said. Please.'

He reaches for my hand and as I fling my arm out to avoid him I knock the bookshelf – a DVD and the spycam dislodge from the shelf and fall to the floor.

Ben sees the little white cube and looks up at me, 'What's that?'

My blood is running cold, 'You know what it is.'

'Have you been?' His voice trails off.

'Yes. I was going to tell you.'

'Even when we?'

'Yes, I wanted it to be candid.'

'But that's creepy, immoral. It's illegal!'

'Well, you know me, I'm not that concerned with those things or who's defining them. If you're going to label me, amoral might be the right word.'

'Manny! What the fuck?'

'I'm not going to use it against you, it's for the project. Do you want copies?'

'No! Delete them!'

'That's complicated. Can we talk about it when you've calmed down?'

'Calmed down? There must be hours of it. Delete it all and show me that you have.'

'OK.'

'This is so wrong.'

The moral thing hadn't crossed my mind. I watch him shaking, he's clearly struggling to think.

After about a minute, he turns to me, 'You've already sent them on to someone haven't you?'

The truth about this right now would fuck the project. I'll put it right when I can.

'Ben, listen. I haven't.'

Chapter 33

I'm standing over Ben, holding a pair of scissors, high on anticipation of today. I lift a lock of his hair and snip.

Ben giggles, 'Feels weird.'

'You said you needed a haircut'

'Can you actually cut hair?'

'It's gonna look cool, you'll see – and if you don't like it we can go suedehead.'

I earned temporary forgiveness for the webcam by giving him the files – on the condition that he will watch the footage first before deciding what should be done with it.

I think about this as I play barber. He still doesn't understand how I could do it and I just can't explain. The whole thing has made me feel even more like I'm different from other people.

I stand the small mirror on the table in front of him. His wavy hair is now roughly lopped and asymmetric, he looks shocked.

I explain, 'It's my interpretation of a classic Bauhaus school cut.'

He grimaces.

I touch his cheek, 'It gives you an energy – atomic – as if you could explode in any direction at any moment. Fucking hot if you ask me.'

I hand him a book from the sideboard , 'From the V&A Modernism exhibition, see page 291. It's a statement, Ben, a new you.'

He stares at the model in the picture, 'Well it is similar in that it's jagged I suppose.' He looks at my uncut hair, covering my eyes and half of my face, 'So do I get to have a go on you?'

'I need to keep this posh public schoolboy look, just for today. People will need to recognise me. Tomorrow, you can give me any style you want.'

'What is it you've organised? Tell me.' he pleads.

'Technically, June has organised it. A surprise, just for you.'

He reaches his hand back and touches my thigh, 'I doubt that, you're plotting.'

I step away playfully, 'Save it sexy. Go and have a shower then it's time to dress up.'

I'm checking myself out in the full length mirror when Ben comes in wrapped in a towel. His eyes widen, 'Wow! This is a special occasion.'

I'm wearing close fitting black trousers and a black stretch-shirt, my hair is combed to perfection. I point to a similar outfit laid out on the bed, 'Your turn.'

He picks up the shirt and feels the fine fabric, 'Where did you get these?'

'Hermes brought them, that's all I'm going to say.'

'With a 30 day returns policy?' He laughs and starts to dress.

I know his body and the clothes fit well. It's hot

that we're in the same stuff – it's like we're in uniform.

'You look stunning, Manny.'

I can see the lust in his eyes. I point to some new black trainers in an open box near the window. Ben looks at my feet 'But you're still wearing those red trainers.'

'Yeah. In honour of something but that's not important right now.'

He takes the new trainers out of the box and starts to put them on.

'Please Manny, where are we going?'

'I'm not telling.'

Chapter 34

Once we set off, it doesn't take him long to work out where we're heading, but he's none the wiser as to why. We walk mostly in silence, there's no point explaining until we get up there.

As we make our way up The Hill, I feel like I'm scanning the land beneath my feet as I walk, its shimmering power surging up into me.

I look across at Ben. Did I need to play with his heart so hard to get to this point? Probably not. He's going to have to pay with an Icarus moment. But when he gets over everything, he'll feel blessed to have met me. And all in all, he's my favourite, my protege even.

As we reach the lower entrance to The Hill, I grab Ben's hand, put my finger to my lips and lead him up. The sun is high in the blue. I think I hear voices but I can't be sure. Finally, we cross the defensive earthwork and step onto the plateau.

Ben gasps and for a moment too, my breath is taken away. The entire summit is scattered with picnickers, way more than the twenty or so groups June had invited. Families and friends are camped on and around richly coloured blankets held down with chill boxes, hampers, food. A champagne cork pops. I recognise one of the old 'ladies' from the patisserie.

The breeze brings us snippets of conversations.

I sweep my arm across the scene, 'I give you the good people of the city.'

Ben stares at me, 'What have you done?'

I try to pull a funny 'What me?' face but it falls flat.

He looks flustered, panicked, 'I don't get it. What's this for? Isn't this illegal? Don't you need a licence or something?'

I stand close behind him, wrap my arms around his chest and rest my chin on his shoulder. 'They just all happen to be here at the same time.'

He struggles a bit but I'm not letting him go.

'So, this is your doing?' he asks.

'Look, I know I didn't consult on this bit of the project, but it's worked and then some! Clearly the news got out and no one was going to miss the social event of the summer.'

Ben looks down at the trampled grass, 'What about the skylarks? Their nesting place.'

I gaze up into the sky, 'Collateral damage.'

He hisses in disgust, 'For what exactly?'

'You'll work it out. Let's walk around to the other side, I need to check something.'

I lead us towards the trig point. I see Cake Bear with some other bears in the distance. When I spot Arran and the Duchess with what looks like a family group – I manoeuvre to the blindside of Ben, I definitely don't want them to notice me.

'So why are we dressed in black?' Ben asks.

I point to the picnickers, 'So that we're invisible,

to them.'

We pass a group sitting around a handsome spread of food on a fuschia blanket. A pink checked guy in his thirties wearing an exclusive polo shirt passes an empty champagne bottle to a sturdy woman with big blonde hair. She kneels up, looks around, notices us and flexes an index finger in our direction and calls out, 'Hello there, are you with the event?'

I tap my chest and look at her questioningly.

She tuts, and speaks more slowly and loudly this time, 'Excuse me, you there, are you staff?'

'Oh goodness, no!' I turn away from her and wink at Ben.

She turns to an identically styled woman sitting next to her, 'Surely we're not expected to take all this back home?'

'Didn't we see a bin near the entrance?' says the guy in the polo shirt.

'Yaahhh. Just the one if I remember. It's going to be full to overflowing later.' replies big blonde woman one.

'The refuse workers will earn their money this week, haah haah haah.' big blonde woman two drawls.

I turn to Ben, 'See, we're staff, servants, invisible unless required. Well, just you wait.'

When we reach the trig point I stop and look towards the car park – it and the lane leading up to it are chock full with parked 4x4s, taking up every bit of verge.

I rub my forehead with my fingers, 'I hope this

'doesn't bring the pigs out just yet.'

'So this is to do with the project. Why this? No, actually, my first question is, 'How?''

I hesitate, weighing up how truthful I should be, 'Your Mum helped me put the list together, then she took it upon herself to call that city magazine and they sponsored it, and you'll love this bit, Yes Sir! delivered the invites.'

Ben's face pales, 'Mum! Does she know what all this is about?'

'I'm sure she does deep down, but it's our project, we carry the can, or I will on my own if need be.'

'You used her.'

'I dare you to tell her that. Anyway, the magazine sponsored the picnic and paid for the invitations. I'm not even sure they know I exist.'

'So this is your action to get one up on Robinson?'

'He said rebellion wasn't possible – he didn't even try, Ben. Even failure takes us beyond the present, beyond the status quo.'

'And so today, you've gathered all these 'good people of the city' together for a solstice picnic. And so what?'

'It's for you and for everyone who feels like an outsider in this city. It just has to be done. Something will come of it.'

'And you, where do you fit in?'

'I don't know. I feel like a different kind of outsider.'

'A special one?'

'Yes, and you know that, if I'm honest.'

'So special you didn't share this plan with me.'

'It's not like that. I wanted it to be a surprise, a gift.'

He looks unconvinced, 'But bringing these people here? You still haven't answered that. Is it symbolic or something?'

I bring him closer and kiss him softly on the lips, 'We're not started yet. Let's go to the middle, it's quieter there. It's going to be alright. Trust me.'

We wind our way through the 'good people' and settle unnoticed into our little hollow. We flop onto our backs and look up at the sky. I let my eyelids close. I feel the sun's heat hitting the blackness of my clothes. I soak up the energy here, at the centre of things.

Ben props himself up on his elbow and looks down at me, 'So what do we do now?'

'We wait - not long now.'

Chapter 35

Snatches of a booming beat, like thunder, silences the wind and thuds through my chest.

Ben jumps up, 'What the hell?'

A voice sweeps across the plateau, 'Say namo, say macquallay, uum eh, uum ah.'

I get to my feet, 'Now for the real action.'

A battered pale green Land Rover appears over the lip of the hill and rumbles onto the plateau – huge sound system speakers strapped to its roof. The 'good people' sit up like rabbits, their dogs freeze mid-pose.

Everything is happening in slow motion. Whatever I've unleashed, I feel it coming up through my feet, making my legs shake, coming from deep in The Hill.

Ben has paled translucent.

Heads appear around the rim of the earthen fortress ditch, rising up, rising up. Unstoppable faces of all seven ages of humankind. Bodies every shape rising up, advancing to the beat – Urban streetwearers, hippy foragers, clapped out Ibiza ravers, hoggers of library seating, babies in onesies, twinks in onesies, new age goddesses, people who get their hands dirty working, bold emo's, daring schoolkids, all swarm into the space. Bottles and cans raised in the air.

Some of the 'good ladies', experienced in taking

control in domestic matters, stride towards my rebellion but it merely flows past them. The 'good ladies' swing around and refocus – corralling their dogs and beef cattle husbands, whilst sweeping up little ones into their arms.

I grab Ben's hand and pull us towards the outer path. Hundreds more happy rebels are pouring up every available track onto The Hill. The lane is blocked with old camper vans.

Ben looks horrified, 'Fuck, Manny, this is going to be war!'

'This space is ours. I wanted to bring them onto our territory. '

'It could get nasty.'

'Not from our side, non-violence is the message. It's a cultural ambush, nothing more, at this stage.'

'And you can guarantee that, right now?'

'I'm just teaching these 'good people' a lesson.'

I hear a baby crying and we both immediately look across. They're OK. Some 'good children' have slipped their parents and are dancing with the kids of the rebellion.

'Why here?' asks Ben.

'I felt it, from the moment I first saw it. And it feels right now. This hill was meant for it. It's such a queer place.'

'You are crazy, you know that, don't you?'

'Maybe. But as a first go at queerscapes action, it's not bad is it?

He shakes his head.

I put an arm around his shoulder, 'Yes, I'm trying to prove myself to Robinson, but I couldn't have done it without you.'

The Land-Rover sound-system comes to a halt, now surrounded by the hundreds strong uprising. Many of the 'good people' have begun a futile retreat. Their blocked-in 4x4s trigger outrage, ignite family arguments, angry gesticulations, the beef cattle are on their phones. Some accept total defeat, and leaving their cars behind, trudge down the footpath back to their city.

I feel a tap on my shoulder and I turn around quickly. It's Tom and his big open smile, holding a half-full bottle of champagne, 'Hey Manny, I've been looking all over for you.'

Tom casts an appraising and appreciative glance at Ben before he speaks again, 'This is some fucking scene. Best thing that's happened round here in years, in fact ever!'

I can feel my chest puffing out.

Tom passes the bottle to Ben, 'Hey, I'm Tom.'

'Thanks, I'm Ben.'

'Ah, The Ben.'

Tom puts his arm around my waist and then pulls Ben onto his other arm, 'Cummon boys it's time to party.'

Chapter 36

Dusk comes so quickly - on what we're on. Whilst we dance, I'm charging up on all the energy these people and The Hill has to offer.

An old guy in combats approaches Tom and whispers in his ear before wandering off again. Tom grabs me and shouts to make himself heard, 'They're looking for the organiser, they wanna pay homage.'

'You know him?'

'Yeah, he's legit.'

'Ok, I just need to have a piss. Wait here.'

I jog down the quietest path till there's no one around. I step closer to a bush and unzip. As I piss, I feel ecstatic. I've done it, Robinson, I've done something! I arc my piss high into the air in victory. I shake my now tumescent cock and turn back towards the uprising. She stands there, The Duchess, just a few feet away, looking down towards me. I hastily stuff my dick back into my pants.

'I thought it was you.' She tilts her head back towards the summit, 'You'll have something to do with this fiasco, no doubt.'

I shrug.

'Puerile nonsense. No matter, I'm here to...' and she raises that bony finger.

I step towards her. 'Here to what?'

'Firstly, keep away from my grandson. I heard what you did, you're deranged. In fact, I suggest you move on from our city. We don't tolerate upstarts like you here.'

That fearless sense of entitlement, it's not gonna work this time.

I laugh, 'Arran, your grandson? He's a big boy now. We go way back, hasn't he told you?'

I brush her aside and start to walk up the path.

She calls out 'Watch it boy - someday soon you're going to bump into some folks who are really going to teach you a lesson.'

I feel the lightning across my face. I step back down towards her, 'Not here they won't.'

She faces me down, 'How can you be sure?'

I reach out and put my finger to her forehead, 'Because this is our space, not yours.'

She stands her ground.

I push on her forehead slowly, 'My domain.' My finger tip feels hot against her cold skin.

Her lower lip trembles.

I push harder on her skull, 'My space - now fuck off.'

She looks over my shoulder and calls out, 'Arran, Frederick, Help!'

I jerk my head and look behind me, there's no-one in sight, just the glow from the happening.

Her resistance disappears from my finger, I hear her footsteps, then a shriek followed by bracken being flattened, a thud on the ground and a dull crack. I turn back to where she was, there's blood on a raised flint nodule next to the path. She's lying next to the bush, my piss still drips from its leaves.

I step in after her. She's still - blood runs out of the back of her head, I check her pulse. Gone.

'You can't do this to me you bitch!' I hiss under my breath. 'It's not happening, you won't sidetrack my project.'

I push her with my foot and she rolls a few feet down the slope, coming to rest under a bank of blackberry bushes, out of sight. I stand there, searching inside myself for that cold part that can hold this. Will hold this. I put it there with the other stuff. Collateral damage.

Chapter 37

Ben and Tom are where I left them. The bass of the drum vibrates through my chest. Tom is dropping a tab onto Ben's tongue. Tom winks at me, 'Wanna crank things up?'

'I've already moved up a gear, honey, but why not.' I reply, sticking my tongue out.

'Way to go.'

'Where's my Man of the Crowd?'

Ben shouts so he can be heard. 'He's over by the sound system somewhere.'

'And is everyone ready for me?'

'Oh yes, bro.'

'Let's find Man of the Crowd first. I want him there.'

The more we push into the crowd, the more I'm recognised – high fives, clicks of fingers, thumbs up. The euphoria floods over what happened back there.

When we reach Man of the Crowd, he's doing some weird walking-a-tightrope dance. He stops when he sees me and with crazy happy eyes pushes me towards the Land Rover.

I clamber up the ladder fixed on the side of the vehicle and onto the roof rack. The crowd roars. I close my eyes and let my energy pulse out across the crowd. Their energy comes back to me and I soar high up into the air - I'm looking down at the light - the airwaves - the heartbeats - pulsing out from My New City. My Homoland.

And I see the other city in the distance - its planned layout, its safe streets, its society spaces, its family designs, its closed doors, its locks – keeping us in check, keeping us irrelevant, keeping us secondary. Our marks on that city are few, one gay bar and a few dusty paths in liminal spaces, everything else is coded. We're expected to blend in and be thankful for the crumbs of virtue signalling. No more.

My eyes are a laser and a purple beam gouges into your world heritage – a fissure that slices through the Crescent, topples the obelisk, breaches the Roman Baths, silences the Abbey bells. We're making our mark.

Night slowly turns to day, Homoland is surrounded by a ring of mist as if The Hill has detached itself from the landscape and is floating up to join me.

Chapter 38

My feet and the ground connect. I look around me, smoke curls from heads into the cool air. The early morning sun takes dew from the long grass. The Land Rover makes its way home through a lower field.

I stumble around looking for my boys. I take out my phone. Man of the Crowd has sent me his footage from yesterday and I forward it to Robinson before calling Ben.

They're all there, in the hollow.

Ben looks up, 'Ah he returns.'

Man of the Crowd is asleep.

Tom is skinning up, 'You were working that crowd girl - we left you to it in the end.'

I snuggle down next to Ben, he seems edgy but doesn't repel me. He takes out his phone, 'Look at this - we made the news.'

My heart is in my mouth, I think about The Duchess, do I need to go on the run already? Her interference has changed everything for me.

The reporter talks to camera, 'This appears to have been an illegal rave that disrupted an organised family event.'

I snarl, 'The 'good people' of the city are already writing the story they want to tell. Robinson was right, it's gonna come to nothing.'

Ben nudges me, 'You're wrong. They won't be as sure of themselves. You're just having a come down.'

Tom stands up, 'We better move on though, the cops will be here soon.'

I lead my proteges down to the brook and we chill there, out of sight.

I can't wait to see the look on Robinson's face when he finds out what I've done here. I've proved you can bring people together, take action. And this is just the start.

As we sit next to the brook under the cover of hawthorn, my mind swirls down into the black water. I imagine myself in a police cell awaiting a duty solicitor. I try to block it out by recalling everything I've done since arriving at Ben's but the arrest nightmare blooms, my solicitor's called Daniel, I tell him truths. How I'd misled people into colluding. I give no reason other than to cause disruption. Fascinated by what happened, he warms to me, but he's an insider, on their side ultimately. And whilst in custody, the Duchess is reported missing - and that a search has begun.

Panic flutters in my chest about police questioning. I think of the other debris in my life which they might dig up - the stuff stored in my cold place

Item 1 – the French boy from West London

Anarchists. I'd followed him all over with my tongue hanging out and when he got a job as a civil servant, he'd been in touch about planning something pretty horrific. I'd backed out but maybe I'd left a trail.

Item 2 is my Nan - well actually her prescription meds that I would sell behind her back, seeing as she never took them. Her choice. She seemed fine until one day she collapsed and died.

And as the hours have worn on, other thoughts are creeping in – that Robinson isn't that impressed. I feel myself shrinking and turning in on myself. I feel weak. I want to go back to The Hill.

Chapter 39

When dusk falls, we go to Ben's, hole up in his bedroom and wait to see what happens. Ben sticks to me like glue and the other two wrap around us.

Robinson happens first - via a text the morning after the morning after.

'Bravo Manny! Another victory for one of my protégés.'

I scroll in disbelief as he follows that with links to various recent news articles – house-sized tagging on the rock face of a legendary beauty spot – the Arts Council finance system hacked and funds reappropriated – iconic books kidnapped from the British Library and being held hostage.

One of my protégés? I crumple. I drag myself into the spare room and video-call him.

He's changed his style. He's wearing an oversized 'Wham' t-shirt that makes him look scrawny. His straggly hair now dyed jet black. His eyes are no longer needy. His smile oozes control.

'Manny.' he says as if he's giving me permission to talk.

'Fuck you! I'm coming for you. I know where you are.'

'Is that so? Berlin's a big place.'

That takes the wind out of me. What's he doing there?

'Come on, Manny, you're in the heat of the moment. Trying to deal with the revelation that this is something bigger than you. Your ego is in free fall. I understand.'

'You've been playing with me all along. Manipulated me. Groomed me.'

'Oh come on, Manny. Don't tell me I manipulated you into doing something you didn't deep down didn't want to do. I have my ways and you have yours, so I hear. And most importantly, these Disruptions, as I call them, have worked a treat. OK, I've applied questionable morals, if any at all. But who are you to call me out on that? I've not broken your heart have I?'

Robinson talks a lot of shit sometimes, but he brought me round, with his buttering up. '– you're the most special – the most amoral – more than my protégé – more like a small god of something.'

Chapter 40

And so we do what Robinson says - stay put and monitor things.

The Hill happening is not traced to us - to them it was just an illegal rave. After a search - they find The Duchess. It's reported that she seems to have died from a fall – no foul play suspected – drunk on champagne, she took the wrong path – misadventure is on the cards.

June, though not unfriendly, seems cautious. She's spent a lot of time in her room.

I'm sitting at the bottom of the garden, just off a call with Robinson. He's been monitoring the city for signs of a revived artistic community of radicals. Good luck with that. The place looks and feels the same to me. The Literature Festival is as middle-of-the-road as ever. The Jane Austen Weekend has taken on a fundamentalist vigour. Robinson is more positive and says it's just a matter of time.

Robinson himself continues his renaissance, citing his move to Berlin as an act of personal disruption; it probably means he's developed some new kinks. I get up from the step and run through what I've just agreed with Robinson.

When I get to our bedroom, they're all there, in the bedroom. Ben at the computer, Tom and Man of the Crowd on the bed.

Ben reads my face immediately, 'What?'

It's a question he already knows the answer to.

'I'm done here.' I say.

Ben throws his hands up, 'Just like that?'

The other two look down at the bed.

His face hardens, 'Done with here or done with me?'

'Here.'

He looks around the room, 'Does anyone else have a say?'

I bring his eyes back to me, 'Should they?'

Ben is almost shaking, 'We sleep in this bed together. I love you, Manny, doesn't that mean anything?'

'You and me means stuff yeah – no need to give it that label.'

'So what now?'

'We talk.'

Chapter 41

Ben and me go to the spare bedroom. He looks resigned. We sit on the bed in silence. I wait for my breathing to calm and his to follow. After a few minutes I'm ready.

'Robinson is in Berlin. He's fallen in with a bunch of writers and artists, all very underground. He likes your writing, he's inviting you to go over and work on something with him.'

Ben looks shocked, I carry on,

'He's developing ideas on how a queer city might look – buildings - homes – streets, the landscape. He lives in a collective out on the east side. He's even found some free German lessons for you.'

Ben seems impressed, intrigued by Robinson, like he always has been.

'So I'm going to be his new protége?' Ben giggles.

'Do you want to be?'

'Maybe.'

'Be prepared. He's a bit of a predator and a perv. Take Tom with you, he's street smart, maybe even Man of the Crowd. You can look out for each other. Robinson says you're all welcome.'

Ben puts his arm gently around my neck, 'And what about you?'

'I'm looking for someone. I might join you later.'

'Is he hot, your next project?' asks Ben with a hint of bitterness.

'I laugh, Yeah. French, blue eyes, doesn't butter his hair, clumsy fighter, dead.'

'What's all that supposed to mean?'

'Sorry.It's a personal thing, you know I'll not tell you, yet.'

He shakes his head in defeat.

'Is it a plan then? Go to Berlin?'

Ben sighs, 'I need to think about it. It's not practical. Mum, you know.'

'I'll sort that. We've been talking.'

'Behind my back?'

'No, just generally.'

I see the red gazelles on the floor by the wardrobe. I kneel down, pick up one of them, loosen the laces and look up at Ben.

'Will you look after these?'

He nods.

I take his left foot and slip the red trainer on.

'You never told me, whose were they before?'

'Ask Robinson, he'll tell you.'